THE CHRISTMAS TRIPLETS

BY
TANYA MICHAELS

MILLS & BOON

First Published in Great Britain 2016
By Mills & Boon, an imprint of HarperCollins*Publishers*
1 London Bridge Street, London, SE1 9GF

© 2016 Tanya Michna

ISBN: 978-0-263-92038-3

23-1116

Our policy is to use papers that are natural, renewable and recyclable products and made from wood grown in sustainable forests. The logging and manufacturing processes conform to the legal environmental regulations of the country of origin.

Printed and bound in Spain
by CPI, Barcelona

"You didn't like me because of 'a vibe'?" Will repeated.

"Sorry," Megan said in a small voice.

He sighed. "I guess I didn't help matters. Every time I saw you, I was determined to get a more positive response. A smile, a laugh, something. I just compounded the problem, didn't I?"

"That's all behind us." She gave him an earnest look, laying her hand on his forearm as she added in an oh-so-sincere tone, "I find you downright tolerable now!"

"Smart-ass."

"Language, William!" Megan jokingly chided.

"Okay, *smartbutt*."

"Hey!" the bearded cashier interrupted, beaming at them and pointing toward the ceiling. "You two are under the mistletoe."

Megan's pulse stuttered and she raised her gaze slowly, as if afraid of what she'd find. Yep. A sprig of mistletoe with a red velvet bow tied around it. Her eyes slid to Will's face. He was looking straight at her, his expression hungry. A hot shiver went through her. *Is he going to kiss me?*

comments came from a habit of trying to rile their opinionated parents, who disapproved of Jace not finishing college and becoming a bartender. "You've had one and a half beers in the last four hours, and you spend half of your nights off with us. Lame."

"About not seeing us again until Christmas," Cole interrupted, "you do realize you're supposed to be my best man in two weeks?"

"Oh, your wedding is *this* month? I completely forgot."

"I know you're kidding," Cole said, "but make any jokes like that in front of my future wife, and I'll find a reason to lock you in the town jail. Kate's a bundle of nerves, worried something will go wrong." As he finished the sentence, his expression turned sheepish, as if he suddenly remembered how wrong Will's own wedding had gone.

Although to say it had gone wrong implied it had actually happened.

Will's fiancée had broken off their engagement the night before they were supposed to get married. He suppressed the humiliating memory, confident Kate and Cole's big day would be perfect. They adored each other; they even loved each other's kids, from Kate's handful of a fourteen-year-old to Cole's twin girls.

"I would never do anything to cause Kate stress," Will solemnly promised. As far as he was concerned, she and her son were already family.

"I know she's excited about the wedding," Cole said, "but it's also bringing up a lot of memories of her late husband. And she's anxious about our trip to Houston this weekend." They were going to the

city so Cole could meet some of her friends and former teaching colleagues—people who'd been part of
her life before her police officer husband was killed
in the line of duty. "Even though everyone's been
supportive, congratulating her on the engagement,
she's nervous about people meeting husband number
two. She debated for hours about inviting her former
parents-in-law to the wedding. They sent a gift, but I
think she was secretly relieved when they said they
couldn't make it."

"All this stress over who to invite and where to
seat them and what to register for?" Jace shook his
head. "If I ever marry, I'm eloping."

"I don't know which is less likely," Will commented, "*you* getting a woman to agree to spend her
life with you or our mother letting you live if you
cheat her out of the wedding."

"Speaking of our mother." Cole stood. "I promised
her I'd be back before the twins' bedtime. So I guess
I'll take my money and run."

Once the door had closed behind Cole, Jace straightened in his chair, looking more serious and alert than
he'd been all night. "Hey, I wanted to talk to you, but
not in front of our brother, the long arm of the law."

Will frowned. "You planning on committing a
crime?"

"It's about Amy."

Oh, hell. Will's stomach sank. He'd befriended
twenty-one-year-old Amy Reynolds after her apartment caught fire. She was a sweet kid, juggling three
jobs while trying to raise a baby, but her on-again,
off-again older boyfriend was bad news. Although
local law enforcement had never compiled enough

Tanya Michaels, a *New York Times* bestselling author and five-time RITA® Award nominee, has been writing love stories since middle-school algebra class (which probably explains her maths grades). Her books, praised for their poignancy and humor, have received awards from readers and reviewers alike. Tanya is an active member of Romance Writers of America and a frequent public speaker. She lives outside Atlanta with her very supportive husband, two highly imaginative kids and a bichon frise who thinks she's the center of the universe.

For Melissa Silva, one of the best friends
anyone could ask for, who moved away
while I was working on this book.
I miss you every day—hope you have
that new guest room ready for visitors!

Chapter One

Ever since Thanksgiving, the flower shop had been selling a lot of poinsettias and wreaths, but the cowboy frowning intently at the chart on the counter was obviously looking for something else. Watching him try to make a selection, Megan Rivers thought suddenly of her ex-husband—of the colorful gerbera daisies he'd brought her when the fertility treatments finally worked and, months later, the overpriced guilt bouquets when he cheated on her during her complicated pregnancy. Was the handsome cowboy who'd wandered in seeking a way to ease his own guilt?

Where's your holiday spirit, Meg? This was supposed to be the "most wonderful time of the year," not the most cynical.

Besides, when the man tipped back his hat for a better look at an arrangement, she recognized him as a local rancher who'd been really kind to her three-year-old daughters at a town festival a few months ago. After a moment of searching her memory, his name came to her. "It's Jarrett, right? Can I help you find something?"

"Yes, please." He gave her a grateful smile. "I'm drawing a blank. Roses for romance, lilies for bereavement. What kind of flower says 'I know your parents make you crazy, but it's just a few days and you're a badass who can handle anything'?"

Megan laughed in spite of herself. She could relate to parental anxiety. Her own mother was…challenging. "Hmm. That's not a request we get every day. But lavender is known to be soothing. We could make sure there's some of that included."

She opened a sample book and flipped through some photos, suggesting changes they could make to personalize each bouquet. A few minutes later, as she was writing Jarrett's contact information on an order form, the bell above the door rang, signaling the arrival of Gayle Trent, the local sheriff's mother.

Megan waved. "Good morning. Here on wedding-related business?" The sheriff was getting married in a couple of weeks, and Megan was responsible for all the arrangements, boutonnieres and pew bows. The bride-to-be had placed the pertinent orders weeks ago, but she wouldn't be the first bride to second-guess details as the big day approached.

Gayle shook her head. "Just picking up the wreath for the quilting club's annual holiday luncheon."

Jarrett turned to enlist her help. "As long as you're here, Mrs. Trent, can I get your opinion on these flowers I'm ordering for Sierra?"

After both Megan and Gayle had assured him his girlfriend would love the arrangement, he bade them a cheerful farewell.

Watching him walk down Main Street through the store window, Gayle snickered. "He is *so* smitten. And who can blame him? Sierra Bailey is gorgeous— and just feisty enough to keep him in line. Watching him dote on her, it's hard to believe he was the town's most notorious heartbreaker."

Avoiding the older woman's gaze, Megan busied herself with ringing up the wreath. She barely knew Jarrett Ross, but as far as she could tell, the biggest heartbreaker in town was her own next-door neighbor—and Gayle's son—Will Trent. Unlike his soon-to-be-married older brother, Will went out with a new woman every week. Megan could admit that the dark-haired firefighter was appealing in a superficial, blue-eyed and flirtatious way, but judging from his romantic habits, he had a shorter attention span than the average preschooler. Was Gayle oblivious to her son's busy dating schedule?

Unlikely. Megan had been here less than a year, but she'd quickly discovered that the town of Cupid's Bow thrived on gossip. Maybe Gayle was choosing willful ignorance.

"That will be thirty-nine dollars," Megan said, hoping the subject of local heartbreakers was officially closed.

But Gayle was still chuckling as she pulled her wallet from her purse. "Good thing Jarrett met Sierra when he did. Eventually, he would have run out of eligible ladies here in town. Although *you* never dated him, did you, dear?"

"No, ma'am." Megan hadn't dated anyone since moving here after her divorce. When would she find the time? There were hardly enough hours in the day to balance her job as a florist with raising triplets. And she wouldn't have gone out with Jarrett Ross anyway, given his reputation. She'd learned her lesson the hard way, married to an incurable flirt who'd had two affairs she'd confirmed and others she'd suspected.

"Well, if you're not seeing anyone," Gayle teased, "maybe we can introduce you to some nice single men at the wedding."

Megan managed not to shudder. "That's sweet, but I have triplets. I barely have the energy to drive to work in the morning, much less try to impress a man." What would she discuss with a bachelor anyway? Her last year had centered on potty training, teaching her kids the alphabet and keeping Daisy— the most adventuresome of her girls—out of trouble.

Parenting wasn't easy, but even at her most exhausted, Megan was grateful for her girls. There had been discouraging days she'd doubted the fertility treatments would ever work. Now she was blessed with three children!

I have my daughters. I don't need a man.

THE PROBLEM WITH playing your brothers at poker, Will Trent decided Thursday night, was that they knew you too well for bluffing to succeed. Earlier in the evening, the cards had been with him, but it seemed his luck had run out.

"That's it." He tossed his crappy pair of fours on the table and eyed his brothers. "Get out of my house. I don't want to see either of you again until Christmas. And I expect you to buy me excellent gifts with the cash you've won off me."

His younger brother, Jace, snorted. "I plan to blow my winnings on liquor and women. Life is a nonstop party."

Will rolled his eyes. His brother's outrageous

evidence to arrest him, there was talk of the man dealing illegal prescription drugs.

"They suspended Amy at work," Jace said. "She was strung out the last two nights she waitressed. She claims she's just jittery after a few sleepless nights with the baby and too much caffeine, but it was obviously more than that. I know the owners don't want to fire her, but she's been breaking glasses and screwing up orders. She misplaced a customer's credit card and spilled a pitcher of margaritas on the mayor's wife during Ladies' Night. Do you think she'd listen if you try to talk to her?"

Will shoved a hand through his hair. "I don't know." The last time he'd tried to talk to her about the baby's father and her own well-being, she immediately became defensive. He could only imagine how hard it was for a barely adult woman to raise a baby alone. It was natural that she would turn to the baby's father for help—but when he broke laws and risked her health? "For her sake, I'll try."

"Be persuasive," Jace advised as he stood. "Use your famous Will Trent charm. It's practically a superpower. No woman can say no to you."

Will didn't bring up the ex-fiancée who'd very effectively said no less than twenty-four hours before their scheduled walk down the aisle, or the cranky neighbor woman who seemed to inexplicably dislike him even though he'd done his best to be likable whenever he saw her. "You sure you shouldn't talk to Amy? The two of you are closer in age."

"I don't know. She had a case of hero worship for you after you helped put out that fire at her apartment complex. If *you* can't get through to her…" Despite

Jace's reputation for being glib and irreverent, there was real concern in his voice.

"I'll talk to her," Will promised. He wasn't sure yet how he'd succeed when his last attempt had failed, but it was the right season for Christmas miracles.

"Good, then I guess I'll be headed out, too. Unless you want some help planning a bachelor party."

"There's not going to be a bachelor party. Cole has been very adamant." He'd cited reasons from upholding the office of local sheriff—hard to keep order if people were whispering about you dancing with a lampshade on your head—to not wanting gossip about strippers to reach the ears of his teenage stepson. Then there was the obvious—Cole was so crazy about Kate that he'd rather spend a free evening with her than scantily clad exotic dancers.

"We could plan one anyway, as a surprise. It doesn't have to be in Cupid's Bow. There's a club in the next county that—"

"Now you're just being sad. There are ways of seeing women naked without slipping ones and fives into their G-strings."

"You would know, Romeo." Jace's tone was a blend of sarcasm and admiration that only a sibling could achieve.

It was true Will had been dating a lot lately. For weeks after being dumped, he'd kept to himself. Then his dad had gently suggested that Will should look at the broken engagement as an opportunity.

You and Tasha got together when you were freshmen in high school. I know you loved her, but you were following through on a future you planned as a kid. Sow some oats. Find out what Will the man wants out of life. Mark my words, son, this may be a blessing in disguise.

Why not? After all, he was single for the first time in his adult life. He owed it to himself to enjoy it as much as possible.

"I'll walk you out," he told his brother. Tomorrow was trash day, and he had bins to roll to the curb. As soon as they stepped onto the porch, Will wished he'd thrown a jacket on over his Cupid's Bow Fire Department T-shirt. "Temperature's dropped."

"Hope it stays cold for the tree lighting this weekend. It never feels as festive when it's eighty-five degrees outside."

Will laughed. "That was an unseasonably warm fluke almost ten years ago. You're just mad Mom made you wear your Christmas sweater anyway." It sure as hell wasn't eighty-five degrees now. He hustled down the steps, trying to keep his teeth from chattering.

Jace's car sat parked in Will's half of the extra-wide driveway. The driveway he shared with next-door neighbor Megan Rivers began at the street between their mailboxes and eventually split in opposite directions, curving into sidewalks that led to each house. As Jace started his car, Will rounded the house to the wooden enclosure where he kept the trash cans to discourage raccoons and other critters from trying to get past the lids. Arms crossed and head ducked against the wind, he was making the return trip from the curb when he heard wheels bumping over pavement at a rapid clip. He glanced up to find Megan coming toward him. Apparently, he wasn't the only one who'd remembered that garbage and recycling needed to be put out before morning.

He raised his hand in an automatic wave just as a frigid gust sliced across his yard and caught the lid on Megan's recycling bin, flinging it open. Crumpled plastic bottles and milk jugs scattered on the pavement.

He was already moving toward her as he offered, "Want some help?"

"No. Thank you," she said tightly.

He scowled. Why on earth wouldn't she welcome assistance to speed up the process? It was dark out, but he could see she wasn't wearing much more than a robe over pajamas. Didn't she want to get back inside where it was warm? "It's no trouble." Actually, it was. *He* wanted to get back inside where it was warm. Valiantly ignoring his own discomfort, he joked, "I'm trying to save my brother the sheriff a trip out here. We have to make sure no one turns you in for littering."

She smashed a handful of debris back into the bin. "I'll take my chances."

Okay. Message received. The stubborn woman could collect her own empty shampoo bottles and juice boxes. As he headed back toward his front door, he found himself glad Jace hadn't been here to witness that exchange. His brother would have laughed that maybe he'd been wrong about the Famous Will Trent Charm.

Was Megan's disdain evidence that Will was losing his touch? That would put a damper on his plans for making the most of bachelorhood. Then again, his last dozen dates had found him plenty appealing.

People like me. Megan Rivers was just the inexplicable exception that proved the rule.

Chapter Two

By Friday night, Will's body ached and the lingering smell of smoke permeated his hair and skin as he drove up to his house. Today had been a live burn training day. An abandoned house near the outskirts of Cupid's Bow needed to be demolished to expand the road to two full lanes, and the town council had given permission for the fire department to burn the building down as an instructional exercise in fighting fires. Will had been one of the supervisors on-site, making sure the fire didn't spread while giving orders to multiple crews throughout the afternoon.

Even though he'd done a quick cleanup at the station house before sharing a pizza dinner with other firefighters and EMTs, he planned on taking a long shower once he got inside. He parked on his side of the driveway and unplugged his phone from the dashboard charger. He'd been thinking about Jace's words last night and how to best approach talking to Amy. After his shower, he would give her a call and invite her to brunch tomorrow. If they were going to have a sensitive conversation about her life choices, he'd rather meet in person, so she couldn't just hang up if she didn't like what he had to say.

He climbed out of the car, taking an appreciative breath of fresh air, and punched the electric lock on his key ring; a chirp came from the car as the alarm set. In a small town like Cupid's Bow, plenty of people left their vehicles unlocked, but when your brother was the sheriff, you were hyperaware of crime. Jace liked to good-naturedly complain that it was impossible to live up to siblings who were a sheriff and firefighter. "With heroes for brothers, there's no way for me to impress our parents unless I become a doctor—and we all know I don't have the brains for medical school."

Frankly, Will thought his younger brother was smarter than he let on. Someday, Jace would find something he was passionate about, and then he was going to surprise a lot of people. In the meantime, he was the town's best bartender and a volunteer fireman. He'd even shown up for an hour of the exercises today. Not long enough to be plagued with sore muscles afterward, Will thought, rubbing the small of his back. He thought wistfully of a woman he'd gone out with a few times who gave excellent massages. But he'd stopped seeing her when she began hinting she'd like a more serious relationship. Why lead her on? After being with the same girl for almost half his life, he was exploring his freedom.

Almost as if the universe was applauding this decision, a text lit up his phone from Leanne Lanier, a gorgeous blonde waitress at the Smoky Pig.

On my way in for dinner to close shift, thinking of you. Stop by and see me if you get hungry.

He considered asking if she wanted to come over after work, but that would be past midnight. So he responded with Can't wait to see you Tuesday.

A date with the beautiful Leanne for the movies next week, tentative plans with longtime friend Anita Drake for dinner this weekend and the independence to make spontaneous decisions without seeking anyone else's approval first. He unlocked his door, whistling. Yeah, freedom had its perks.

MEGAN SLUMPED AGAINST the kitchen counter, enjoying the first moment of true peace and quiet she'd had in over twenty-four hours. As she waited for the water to boil so she could fix her usual cup of soothing chamomile tea, she had a fleeting urge for something stronger to drink. *Oh, please—you're so exhausted that half a glass of wine would knock you into a coma.* And no matter how drained she was, she couldn't afford to go to sleep yet. Quite a few of Megan's work hours were spent at home in her favorite yoga pants.

When she first moved to Cupid's Bow to work for her semiretired distant relative Dagmar Jansen, Megan hadn't been sure how she'd balance her career with child care. The girls were in a preschool program at a local church that only kept them busy until two in the afternoon. Luckily, for reasons ranging from allergies to wanting lasting keepsakes, a number of Megan's clients wanted silk arrangements and wedding bouquets. She worked on those and on her side business of seasonal gift baskets with supplies she kept in a spare bedroom.

Tonight, she was behind schedule because all of her planned productivity yesterday evening had been shot to hell by Iris's stomach bug. It had been a grueling night.

During one of the lulls between Iris's bouts of vomiting, Megan had been about to take a much-needed shower when she suddenly remembered the trash. Not wanting to go out in the cold afterward with wet hair—the last thing they needed was for her to get sick, too—she'd grabbed a pair of pajamas off the top of her clothes hamper, cinched a robe around herself and hauled ass to get the cans to the curb, hoping none of her neighbors were out and about this late.

So, naturally, she'd been doomed to run into Cupid Bow's Casanova.

She shouldn't care what Will Trent thought of her—it wasn't as if *she* had such a high opinion of *him*. But it was galling to encounter a man who was usually seen with the prettiest women in town while she herself was a half-dressed mess who quite possibly smelled like puke. Maybe turning down his help and chasing him off hadn't been her most courteous moment, but her nerves had been shot after hours of trying to calm Iris's stomach and reduce her fever.

Luckily, Iris seemed to be feeling better today—worn-out but fever free. Megan had watched her other daughters intently to see if anyone else showed symptoms of illness. *So far, so good.* Maybe her manic disinfecting measures had been effective.

And now, thank God, all three girls were asleep. As tired as Megan was, she'd managed to feed and bathe them *and* survive the bedtime ordeal, which had included reading stories, saying prayers, checking for monsters, procuring glasses of water and chaperoning four separate potty trips—by the time her two sisters had gone, Lily swore she needed to try again. Finally, Megan's time was her own.

In a perfect world, she could curl up with a good book or watch something on her television that didn't involve singing cartoon characters. But at least she enjoyed her work. As much as she needed to accomplish, maybe she should skip the chamomile and pick a caffeinated tea.

She was pouring water over a bag of green tea when headlights approached on the street outside.

But then they cut off while the car was still in motion, making her frown. A person cruising around with no lights on after dark was suspicious. Was a thief casing the neighborhood? She watched as the vehicle slowly rolled up to the curb in front of her neighbor's house and a figure climbed out. The streetlight several houses down gave off enough illumination for Megan to see that the person creeping toward Will's house was a curvy woman.

Of course. A woman going to Will's was no surprise—honestly, the man should just install a revolving door—but the cloak-and-dagger secrecy was bizarre. Was this woman involved with someone else and therefore didn't want to risk being seen with Will? Even after her being divorced more than two years, the thought of infidelity made Megan grind her teeth.

She turned away from the window, reminding herself that this was her tranquil time. Memories of being cheated on were not conducive to tranquillity. Besides, she had no interest in her neighbor's sordid affairs.

But just as she exited her kitchen, the pulsating

blare of a car alarm cut through the night. She whirled around to see the woman straightening from Will Trent's car, a package in her hand. The woman stood momentarily frozen, as if unsure how to proceed, but when the alarm continued to sound, she hustled toward her own car and drove away.

Meanwhile, Will's car continued its assault on every pair of ears in the neighborhood. Megan rubbed her temples, thinking that surely he would silence the alarm, but when she heard Daisy wail, "Mama?" she knew that her fleeting chance at serenity had passed.

As soon as Will turned off the spray of hot water, he became aware of the discordant blast of a car alarm and pounding on his front door. Had he been the victim of attempted theft? He tied a bath sheet around his waist and strode toward the front of the house with his car keys in hand. When he opened the door, pointing the key ring at his car to stop the alarm, he was startled to find Megan Rivers on his porch.

Her aloof manner sometimes gave him the impression she wouldn't voluntarily talk to him even if her roof was on fire and he was standing ten feet away with a hose. But she didn't look aloof now. Her face was contorted in fury, her posture battle-ready and her eyes narrowed. Yet, as soon as she got a good look at him, she recoiled, those pale blue eyes widening.

"You… You're not wearing any clothes!" Her gaze traveled down his damp abs to the top of his towel, then abruptly back to his face.

"Well, no. I usually don't while I'm in the shower. Do you do it differently?" he teased, momentarily forgetting that humor bounced off this woman's invisible force field.

"You were showering. So that's why you let your car alarm go on so long?"

"Yeah. I didn't hear it over the water." Her oddly suspicious tone registered. "Why would you think I was deliberately letting it go off?"

Color stained her cheeks, rosy in the glow of the front porch light. "I, uh, thought perhaps you were choosing to ignore it because you were, um, otherwise occupied."

It took a moment for her meaning to sink in. "Why, Ms. Rivers. You have a dirty mind."

"I do not! But everyone in town— Never mind." She shook her head, regaining her composure. "I apologize for storming over here. I worked hard to get my girls to sleep. Then when that stupid alarm startled them and wouldn't stop… I'd better get back to them." She held up the monitor in her hand, and he could hear distant sounds of a cartoon. "I left them with a movie on so that the alarm wouldn't be so jarring in our quiet house, and now I have to redo an extensive tucking-in routine."

He winced. He'd heard his brother complain about how hard it was to get the twins to bed more than once. Triplets had to be even more difficult. "I am truly sorry the alarm woke them. I don't know why it went off, but—"

"I believe one of your lady friends was trying to surprise you with a gift and didn't expect the car to be locked. Please ask her not to do it again—assuming you can figure out which one it was," she said icily.

Will's eyebrows shot up. Where did she get off being so judgmental about his private life?

"I'll send out a group text," he said, annoyed into uncharacteristic sarcasm. She gave him a look so withering he was half tempted to check beneath his towel and make sure nothing had permanently shriveled. Then she spun on her heel and descended the stairs. As she marched across her own lawn, it occurred to him that the exchange was the longest conversation they'd had since she moved in.

"Nice chatting with you, neighbor," he muttered under his breath. "Let's do this again real soon." Like, maybe, the nineteenth of never.

Chapter Three

Thank God for chocolate. As Megan taste-tested one of the brownie balls she'd made for the triplets' day-care teachers, her mood lifted. But then it sank slightly under the weight of guilt as she stared out the kitchen window and recalled her shrewish behavior last night. She'd panicked at having her hard-won peace disturbed, but, after sleeping on it, she could admit that Will hadn't technically done anything wrong. *He* wasn't the one who'd set off the alarm.

His biggest crime seemed to be inspiring insanity in women—first in the locals who threw themselves at him and…for a few minutes last night, in Megan. She'd been flummoxed by the sight of him shirtless and had overcorrected with hostility. If any of her clients heard her use that bitchy tone, the flower shop would be in serious trouble. The Trents were well respected in this town, and several of Will's family members were paying customers. She should apologize—not that he'd exactly been Prince Charming with his snarky boast about group texts.

But this was the season of goodwill. Perhaps she could take him a few holiday treats as a truce? Nothing so grandiose that he might mistake her for one of the women in town who swooned over sapphire eyes and sculpted biceps, just a token offering that said, "I'm not a complete harpy."

Sure. She was a big enough person to manage that.

An hour later, after she and the girls had done some significant sampling of today's holiday baking, she zipped them into their coats and herded them out to the van. She'd pulled aside a few treats for Will but faltered when she saw the strange car on his half of the driveway.

In the place of his usual vehicle sat a beat-up compact with mismatched doors and a dented bumper. Did he have company? Whatever the case, she should deliver this chocolate before she changed her mind.

She buckled the girls into their safety seats. "You three stay put a second. Mommy's going to take these across the driveway to Mr. Trent."

"Mr. Trent wif the noisy car?" Daisy screwed up her face, her expression a clear indictment of their neighbor.

"Yes. And then we'll make our deliveries and visit the library. Okay?"

The triplets chorused their agreement, and she strode toward Will's porch. A woman much slighter than Will's alarm-triggering visitor last night sat huddled on the top step. As she got closer, Megan saw that this visitor was crying.

Megan hesitated. Now what? She didn't want to embarrass the other woman by witnessing her vulnerable moment, but Megan had shed enough tears over a man that she felt a tug of sympathetic kinship.

"Hello?"

The woman raised her head, her freckled face

much younger than Megan had been expecting. Even more disturbing than her youth was the baby sleeping in the car seat next to her. Was the girl even twenty? Surely, Will hadn't…

"Hi," the teary female said. "I'm Amy."

"Megan." She felt a surge of protectiveness toward the young mother. "I live next door."

"Do you know…" Hiccuping, she brushed a tear away from her cheek. "Do you know when Will is coming back?"

"No. Sorry, I don't." Was he even now on a date somewhere while this girl sat here crying over him? "Are you going to be warm enough, waiting out here?"

"The cold is the least of my problems," she said bleakly. But then she mustered a smile as she glanced toward the sleeping infant. "And he has all his cozy blankets and his little hat." It was a fuzzy blue knit cap, embroidered with a smiling koala bear. "Baby clothes are so adorable, don't you think? Adorable, but expensive." Fresh tears welled in her eyes.

Was she here to ask Will for money? Did he bear financial responsibility for the baby? *You shouldn't rush to conclusions.* Still, if it quacked like a womanizing duck and waddled like a womanizing duck…

"Here." Megan passed the girl the tissue paper bundle that had been tied with festive curling ribbon. "To eat while you're waiting."

Amy frowned in confusion. "You came to give these to me? You don't even know me."

"Think of me as your secret Santa," Megan said with an attempt at holiday cheer. Amy might not have been the intended recipient, but Megan no longer felt as if her neighbor deserved the soul-brightening benefits of chocolate.

Quite the contrary. If her grim suspicions were true, what he deserved was to be run out of town.

WILL DIDN'T RECOGNIZE the appalling junk heap of a car in his driveway, but as he pulled up to the house, he was pleasantly surprised to see Amy Reynolds sitting on the top porch step. Since she hadn't responded to either of the voice mails he'd left, he'd worried that she didn't want to talk. Maybe she'd just been too busy to call back. Three jobs and a baby couldn't leave her with much downtime. Sliding the gearshift to Park, he considered enlisting his mother's help. Gayle Trent knew everyone in Cupid's Bow. If she could help Amy find a better paying position, the poor kid could cut back on some of her hours.

As he walked toward the porch and got a closer look at Amy's face, some of his relief to see her faded. Had she been crying?

"Hey," he called, keeping his tone light. "I guess you got my messages?"

She nodded. He couldn't see her expression as she turned away, gently rocking the car seat next to her, but he heard her sniffle before asking, "Is this a bad time?"

"Not at all. In fact, you're just in time for supper," he improvised. This was earlier than he normally ate, but good food eased difficult situations. Plus, if they were in the middle of a meal, there was less risk of Amy bolting as soon as the conversation turned uncomfortable. He wasn't much of a chef, as the crew at the station house frequently liked to remind him, but luckily his mom had sent him home with half a lasagna earlier in the week. If there was ever a cooking competition that involved reheating leftovers, Will would be a serious contender. "Have you eaten yet?"

"Just some chocolate that friendly Megan from next door gave me."

Friendly? Megan? He had a memory of her scowling at him in the porch light last night.

Amy's stomach rumbled, and her cheeks reddened.

"Come in and have dinner. You'll be doing me a favor—I hate to eat alone." When she still looked undecided, he added, "You and the little guy will be good company."

She stood, lifting the car seat, then reached awkwardly for a large duffel bag. It seemed closer in size to a suitcase than a standard-issue diaper bag, but what did he know about how much equipment a baby required? Now that his nieces were in first grade, he enjoyed taking them horseback riding or to see occasional movies, but during their infant years, he'd left the babysitting to his parents.

"Here, let me." He hefted the bag by the strap. The dang thing was heavy, which was saying something, given that Will had to wear sixty-pound gear in his line of duty. Balancing the weight against his hip, he unlocked the door and led her inside.

"Your place is nice," she said shyly.

"Thanks." The front entrance opened into his living room, which was clean, if not fancy. There weren't many decorative touches, but a comfy sectional sofa faced a respectably sized flat-screen TV.

Pausing just long enough to dump the diaper bag on the coffee table, he strolled into the kitchen beyond.

Amy set the car seat on the table, then slumped into one of the chairs, her posture defeated.

He desperately wanted to help but wasn't sure where to begin. "Can I get you something to drink?"

"Just water. Thanks."

When he brought her the glass, he nodded toward the baby who was still snoozing. "Sound sleeper."

"Yeah." Affection lit her gaze, and her lips quirked in an almost smile. "He's great. But he wakes up cranky."

"Hardly a character flaw. I've been known to roll out of bed grumpy myself." He crossed the small tiled kitchen to preheat the oven, then pulled the lasagna pan from the fridge. "Jace told me about what happened at work. About your suspension." When she sucked in a breath, he backpedaled. "But we don't have to talk about it if you'd rather not."

"It's okay. It's past time I talk to someone." Her expression was bleak, but her tone was determined. "I need help, Will."

She looked so lost that he automatically responded, "Anything." Her willingness to admit she was struggling was a damn good sign. He'd anticipated defensiveness and denial. Instead, she was being smart about this, and he wanted to encourage her. "I can't work miracles, but I have a halfway decent head on my shoulders. Plus, lots of people in this town owe me favors. If the two of us try, I bet we can come up with some solutions."

Her bottom lip trembled. "People may owe you— Will Trent, local hero—but no one owes me a thing. I got myself into this mess. I can't completely regret my relationship with Donovan, not when the result was Tommy, but… You've heard the rumors about Donovan? I'm talking to you as a friend," she added quickly. "Not as the sheriff's brother."

Will hesitated. Donovan Anders was a lowlife, and Cupid's Bow would be better off with him in jail. But his main focus right now was helping Amy, not pressing for details that would help his brother build a case. "I've heard gossip."

"Most of it is true," she said, not meeting his gaze. "He told me that he wanted to help, wanted to give me more energy to enjoy my time with Tommy. So I've been taking these…supplements."

Will bit the inside of his cheek, not voicing his opinion of the man who'd taken advantage of a young woman almost a decade his junior. They both knew she wasn't talking about a daily dose of vitamin C. "Amy, the kind of supplements Donovan deals have very dangerous side effects."

Her eyes shimmered with tears. "I'm a horrible mother. I tried to stop, and I can't. If I loved my son enough, wouldn't it be easy? I should be able to stop for Tommy."

"Amy." He sat in the chair next to her, reaching across to squeeze her hand. "Even the best mothers in the world make mistakes. Just don't tell *my* mother I said so," he added with a comical grimace. "That woman still terrifies me."

Amy managed a watery laugh. At the sound, baby Tommy twisted in his car seat, face scrunched in warning. Will expected the infant to join his mother in crying, but then Tommy stilled.

"I need a clean break from Donovan," she said

quietly. "But in a town this size, it's so hard to stay apart."

Will understood. It had been a relief when his ex finally moved out of town because, up until then, he'd felt like he tripped over her every time he left the house. "Anything's possible with enough moral support. You just need a…task force of first responders. People you can call before you slip back into unwanted habits or find yourself facing temptation."

"You make it sound simple."

"It won't be." He wanted to offer encouragement, not false hope. Amy had some serious challenges ahead.

"No." She sighed, watching her now fidgeting son with an unreadable expression. "No, it won't be. But I have to do what's best for him, right?" She sniffed. "I'm leaking all over your kitchen. I should go wash my face. And there's some stuff of Tommy's in my car I need to get."

More stuff? What could she possibly need that wasn't already crammed in that tote? He'd seen blimps over football stadiums that were smaller. But he nodded supportively. "Okay. That'll give Tommy and me a few minutes for some male bonding."

"He'll be awake in a second. Can you hold him so he's not scared, waking up in a strange place?"

"Uh, sure." He entered burning buildings for a living; he'd ridden bulls in junior rodeo. Surely he could pick up a baby and keep him comforted for the few moments it would take for Amy to return.

She swallowed hard. "Will, I don't know what I'd do without your friendship. I…" Shaking her head, she hurried from the room as if afraid of losing her composure. A moment later, the front door shut, startling Tommy from his sleep.

As promised, the baby *did* wake up cranky. In fact, his eyes were barely open before he let loose a wail they could use to part traffic during emergencies. Will was surprised the kitchen walls didn't shake.

Fingers mentally crossed that picking up the baby would quiet him, Will reached into the car seat. The latches on the safety harness turned out to be trickier than he anticipated—or maybe it was only the thrashing, crying baby that made them seem complicated. Either way, after a few fumbled attempts and some nonsensical pleading, Will managed to free the squalling infant. He held Tommy upright, but aside from supporting his head—was the baby young enough that he even needed head support?— Will wasn't sure how to proceed.

"Your mama is coming back," he promised. "I know I'm not who you were looking for, but I swear I'm a decent guy." This did not appease the baby, who only cried louder. "I feel ya, kid. An incompetent bachelor is no substitute for a pretty young woman." At some point, he'd started patting the baby on the back. Tommy wasn't getting any quieter, but at least he wasn't noticeably louder—if that were even possible.

Will paced the kitchen, still patting as if his eardrums depended on it. Over the din, he called, "Amy? My holding him isn't doing the trick." It was a stupid thing to point out, considering that she could hear the baby. Folks in the neighboring town of Turtle could probably hear the baby. Still, desperation reduced him to stating the obvious.

Long moments passed with no response.

Desperation escalated to panic. This much crying couldn't be good for the kid. "Amy?" Pause. *"Amy?"* His heart raced. Was she okay? There was no telling what drugs Donovan had been feeding her, or what physical effects she might be suffering.

He headed toward the restroom, but the door stood ajar. She wasn't in there. Outside, then? Did she need help unloading Tommy's stuff from the car?

Will opened the front door, then stood paralyzed, unable to process what he was seeing. Or, more accurately, *not* seeing—namely, Amy's car.

Dread churned in his stomach. "Oh no, no, no, no." Where her car had been parked, there now sat a small box next to a folded heap of plastic and mesh. Some kind of portable crib, if he wasn't mistaken, with a note taped to it on bright yellow stationery.

Dear Will,
This is the hardest thing I've ever asked anyone, but you're the only real-life hero I've ever met. I know Tommy will be safe with you. I have to get clean for him. I have an aunt who's been through rehab, and she got me a place in the clinic near her. During the weeks I'm gone, I need someone to watch Tommy. My mom might seem like the obvious choice, but she barely knew what to do with her daughter. She was relieved when I started dating Donovan, so he could take care of me. I'll be back soon and will be forever in your debt. Please, please keep him safe for me and tell him every day that his mommy loves him.
Amy

Shock jolted through Will, and a word escaped his lips that he had no business saying in front of a baby. He was reeling too violently to censor himself. When Amy had told him she needed his assistance, he'd unthinkingly vowed, "Anything."

But he sure as hell hadn't expected this.

Chapter Four

Holding Tommy tight against him with one arm, Will used his free hand to drag the crib into the house. The entire time, his head throbbed, and his stomach buckled like he had the worst hangover in history. Tommy's angry cries only added to the pounding in his skull.

"Look, kid, I'm begging for mercy here. You win—my brothers were never able to get me to say uncle when we were growing up." His brothers. Should Will call one of them? After all, Cole had plenty of experience with young children, and it had been Jace who suggested Will reach out to Amy in the first place.

But Cole had left for Houston with his fiancée yesterday. And Jace, who made some of his best bartending tips on Saturdays, was probably working. Which left Gayle Trent. He fumbled his cell phone out of his pocket while trying to find some sort of rocking motion that would pacify Tommy. He had to turn the volume all the way up to hear his mother's phone ring, but, unfortunately, there was no answer. He hung up before leaving a message. The situation seemed a bit too complicated to sum up after the beep.

"All right, we can do this," he told the baby. "But

you're going to have to work with me, Tommy." Didn't babies mostly eat and sleep? Since the kid had already napped, it stood to reason he was hungry. Will just had to strap him back into the car seat long enough to figure out what to feed him. Probably not lasagna.

Milk? Formula? Baby food? "Let's get you buckled safely into your chair so I can see what your mama left us." No doubt the massive duffel bag was packed with supplies. But when he attempted to put Tommy back in his seat, the baby arched his back and went rigid, protesting so loudly that his face turned purple.

"Hey, none of that, now," Will coaxed. "I have a next-door neighbor who specifically asked me to keep it down over here. You wouldn't want to get your uncle Will in trouble, would you?" Thinking of Megan filled him with a sudden reckless hope. She managed three daughters all by herself. Surely she'd know what to do about one crying baby?

You're forgetting, she hates you.

True. But maybe her maternal instinct would kick in when she saw Tommy, and she'd help anyway.

"Mama?"

Megan glanced up just in time to catch the cordless phone. Daisy didn't always wait to make sure recipients had a grip on whatever she was handing them before letting go.

"Gammy!" Daisy said as she toddled out of the kitchen, blissfully unaware of how much Megan did not want to speak with her mother.

Since Daisy had so helpfully answered the phone, it was too late to pretend not to be home. Megan hadn't even heard it ring over the mechanical whirr of the food processor. She'd been shredding broccoli into pieces too small for the girls to pick out of tonight's macaroni and cheese. Whether the broccoli smithereens were big enough to actually add any nutritional value was debatable, but sometimes the best you could hope for in motherhood was a moral victory.

Frankly, daughterhood was no picnic, either. "Hello?" she said, pasting a smile on her face in an attempt to sound cheery and welcoming.

"I can't believe you let a three-year-old answer the phone."

"I'm sure Daisy thought she was being helpful. I was busy getting dinner ready."

"Too busy to speak to your mother?"

Yes. The word hovered on her tongue, but Megan knew she'd never say it. The lasting drama of Beth Ann's hurt feelings wouldn't be worth the short-term satisfaction. "What do you need, Mom?"

"The chance to apologize, for starters. I never should have discouraged you from divorcing Spencer. That man is a no-good cheat."

Megan blinked, stunned by her mother's sudden about-face. After Spencer's first affair, Beth Ann had defended her son-in-law, saying he'd acted rashly in his panic over impending fatherhood and had only succumbed to temptation because Megan was on bed rest and unavailable for "marital relations." Wanting to believe his infidelity was a onetime mistake, Megan had agreed to stay with him on the condition that they see a therapist. But less than a year later, she'd caught him in another affair and left him. Her mother had argued vehemently, claiming Megan was insane to try to raise triplets by herself and that she would regret her decision.

Not as much as I would have regretted setting the example for my girls that it's okay for a husband to be unfaithful.

And now, two years later, her mother was randomly offering her support? "I accept your apology," she said cautiously.

"When I urged you to stay with him, I was only thinking of your well-being. I know how hard it is to raise a child alone." Her own husband, a soldier, had been overseas for much of their marriage. Then, while Megan was in high school, he'd died of a heart attack in his sleep. "But your situation is different than mine. I was almost fifty when Jeremy left me widowed. You're young enough to remarry."

Ah. So that was why Beth Ann was suddenly okay with the divorce—she thought Megan should start searching for Spencer's replacement. *No, thank you.* "I'm glad you've made your peace with the divorce." She ignored the other half of what her mom said. "Maybe we can talk later in the week? If I don't concentrate on the girls' dinner, I may end up burning something."

"If you were married, your husband could keep an eye on the stove long enough for you to chat with me."

Yeah, *there* was great incentive to look for a man—more phone calls like this one. "Mom, I—" A discordant gonging sounded through the house, its warble reminding her that she needed to get her doorbell fixed. "There's someone at the door."

"Uh-huh." Beth Ann's skepticism was palpable. "Well, I'll just call back at a more convenient time."

By the time Megan set down the phone, Daisy was standing on her tiptoes at the baby gate, trying to get a glimpse of who might be outside, and Lily had dashed into the kitchen to cling to her mother. Meanwhile, Iris—very focused for a preschooler—remained on the kitchen floor and continued to color a picture.

Megan distracted anxious Lily with a sippy cup, then stepped over the gate to answer the door, fully expecting someone who would try to sell her lawn care or aluminum siding. Salesmen had a knack for always interrupting right at dinnertime. Still, whoever this person was, he had helped free her from a conversation with her mother, so she was prepared to be friendly as she sent him away. She opened the door, keeping the screen door shut between them, and her mouth dropped open at the sight of Will Trent, holding a ginormous bag and one seriously unhappy baby.

The red-faced infant bore little resemblance to the sleeping cherub she'd seen that afternoon, but she recognized the knit hat with the cute koala. Amy's son. In certain circumstances, an attractive man holding a baby would be adorable. But since the baby was loudly broadcasting his displeasure and the man in question was Will Trent...

"Can we come in?" he asked.

Preferably not. "Where's Amy?"

"Visiting an aunt. Tommy will be staying with me for a while." His expression and stiff body language told her how much he resented the circumstances even before he muttered, "She didn't give me much choice in the matter."

Despite her earlier suspicions, Megan hadn't wanted to believe he was the baby's father. He was older and more worldly than that vulnerable young woman. Men were scum. *Not all of them.* She forcibly reminded herself of Jarrett Ross, who'd been so sweet with her daughters at the fall festival, and Sheriff Cole Trent, a man of integrity who clearly adored his fiancée. Unfortunately, Will's resemblance to his brother seemed to be strictly physical.

"I could use a hand. Please, Megan." It wasn't his pleading tone that got to her, but the baby's pitiful sobs. Tommy was running out of steam, his cries now more bewildered than furious. He seemed perplexed as to why his mother had left him with Will. Biological bond or not, there had to be better babysitters in Cupid's Bow. Of course, after what Amy had said about expenses, maybe she couldn't afford to hire one.

With a sigh, Megan opened the screen door. "Last night it was the car alarm during bedtime. Tonight you've caught us right at dinner. Maybe tomorrow you can park the fire truck outside the house with sirens blaring at bath time."

He gave her a sheepish grin. "Is that your way of saying that life next door to me is never boring?"

Refusing to be sucked in by his humor and aw-shucks charm, she reached for the baby. "When was the last time you fed him?"

"Technically, never."

Her eyebrows shot skyward. "You've never helped Amy feed him?"

"Until today, I've barely even held him." He said it without a trace of shame, reminding her of Spencer. For all that her ex claimed to love his daughters, he preferred absentee fathering, only seeing them on rare occasions like his upcoming holiday visit. He'd scheduled his own children for an early Christmas so that he could spend Christmas Day with his current girlfriend.

"But I'm a fast learner," Will added. "I'm sure I'll get the hang of this in no time."

"Right, because parenting is *such* a piece of cake." She snuggled the baby against her shoulder, feeling sorry for him. *You deserve better.*

"Well, obviously not. I—"

"Do you know when the last time he ate was?" she asked, reframing her original question.

"At least an hour or so?" His hesitant tone made it sound like a guess. "I wanted to put him in the car seat and look in his bag for formula, but the way he was thrashing around…"

From behind her, Daisy asked, "Who baby?"

Megan wasn't sure if her daughter was inquiring who the baby was or who he belonged to. She pointed to Will, aware that it had been a long time since the girls had seen a man in the house. "This is Mr. Will, our neighbor, and *this* is Baby…?"

"Tommy," Will supplied.

Daisy crinkled up her nose. "Tommy's noisy." She turned to pick up her own baby doll from the floor behind her and showed it to Will. "I have quiet baby."

"You're obviously better at this child-care gig than I am." Will set the duffel bag down in the foyer and unzipped it. "Maybe you can teach me a thing or two."

"Lesson number one," Megan said, "feed the hungry baby." Spotting a canister of formula and an empty bottle, she swatted Will's hand out of her way. But she couldn't make dinner for Tommy and feed her girls at the same time. "How are you with macaroni and cheese? Someone needs to get back to the stove, preferably before something catches fire."

He grinned. "The good news is, in case of disaster, the fire department is already here."

"Save the megawatt smile for someone who's not immune and go check on the food. Daisy, can you show Mr. Will our kitchen?" She followed right behind them, making sure Lily didn't panic at the sight of a stranger in the house. The last triplet to be born, Lily had been more timid than her sisters from day one; she also spoke less, struggling with many of her consonant sounds.

"There's baked chicken in the oven," Megan said. "Mitts are hanging on the wall behind the sink. And you need to stir the broccoli bits into the cheese—"

"Broccoli? In macaroni and cheese?" His expression was appalled, mirroring the grimace on Daisy's small face. "Remind me never to have dinner here."

"Don't worry. I wasn't planning to issue any invitations."

JACE WOULD BE SO *disappointed in me*. Where was the fabled Trent Charm? Will should be falling all over himself thanking his neighbor, not criticizing her cooking decisions. It was none of his business if she wanted to screw up perfectly good mac and cheese with broccoli, but Will wasn't at his best right now.

Obviously, he hadn't adjusted to the shock of Amy leaving the baby with him, but it was more than that. He was flummoxed by Megan's continued hostility. *Save the megawatt smile for someone who's not immune*. No woman had ever snapped at him for smiling. It would be easy to assume the brunette was tart and hostile by nature—but she was working with Kate and Cole on the wedding and they both liked her. Amy had called her friendly.

He was curious enough that he almost asked about her "immunity" toward him, but he wouldn't risk antagonizing her while she was giving him much-needed assistance with the baby. Instead, he turned his focus from Megan's weird personality quirks to the kitchen surrounding him. Her counters were covered with far more supplies and appliances than his; he got by with a coffeemaker and microwave. And the room was a riot of color, from the plastic place mats on the table to the yellow curtains framing the kitchen window to the crayoned drawings displayed on the refrigerator with magnets. In fact, one of Daisy's sisters was at his feet, coloring another sheet of paper, reminding him of his niece Alyssa, who was never without art supplies.

"Nice picture," he said to the girl. There were several people-shaped blobs, one covered in red slashes. It reminded Will vaguely of a Mafia movie he'd once seen, but since this was December... "Santa Claus?"

The girl nodded happily.

Watching this exchange, Daisy suddenly declared, "I draw a picture, too!" She plopped on the floor and grabbed a crayon. Her sister shrieked in protest. Meanwhile, the other triplet watched from under the kitchen table, wide-eyed, as she sucked her thumb. As Megan restored peace and sent the girls to wash their hands, he hurried to the stove, hoping that cheesy pasta would soothe tempers.

Will couldn't help noticing that even though

Tommy still hadn't been fed, Megan had done an enviable job soothing him. "He likes you. A lot more than he likes me."

"Babies sense tension." She scooped formula into a bottle. "When you showed up on my doorstep, you were practically rigid with panic. The more relaxed and calm you are, the more he will be."

The uptight brunette was telling *him* to be more laid-back? "Maybe you should take some of your own advice."

"What's that supposed to mean?"

What are you doing, dumb-ass? Charm had gone completely out the door. "Well, to tell the truth, you're a little…prickly."

"Just because I don't fawn over a pair of broad shoulders and blue eyes—" In her arms, Tommy let out a cry. "Sorry, sweetie. Here you go." Her tone switched to soft and crooning. Tommy lunged for the bottle and was making hearty slurping noises within seconds.

Keeping her voice low, Megan asked, "I don't suppose you know how many ounces he normally takes?"

"No clue."

"How much does he weigh?"

Doubting that "heavier than a sack of potatoes" was the answer she wanted, Will shrugged.

She sighed. "How old is he?"

He leaned down to get the baked chicken while doing some mental calculations. "Five months, give or take."

"You're unbelievable." Her glare was hotter than the inside of the oven. "Were you even there when he was born?"

"Of course not. That would— Wait! You don't think he's *mine*?"

Megan blinked. "It seemed logical, since Amy left him with you. And given your—" her face went bright red "—social habits."

Unreal. If it had been up to him, he'd be married right now—perhaps with an actual baby of his own on the way—but this near stranger had him painted as some sort of depraved sex addict. "Lady, you don't know the first thing about me." Unlike Donovan Anders, Will didn't seduce nineteen-year-olds.

"I—" She was interrupted by her daughters rushing back into the room.

"Hands clean," Daisy declared, the entire front of her long-sleeved shirt soaked with water.

Megan pinched the bridge of her nose. "This is really not my night."

Will felt a wave of commiseration. "If it helps, I know exactly how you feel."

"It doesn't." She met his gaze, giving him the first real smile he'd ever seen from her. "But thank you."

Chapter Five

Although Megan would normally admonish Daisy to eat more and talk less, tonight she was grateful for her daughter's chatty presence. Even Iris, excited about their outing to the town's Christmas tree lighting tomorrow, contributed to the dinner conversation, helping mask what would've been an awkward silence between Megan and Will. *I misjudged him.* She needed to apologize for her rash assumption, but it seemed like bad parenting to discuss his sex life in front of the girls.

She'd invited Will to stay for dinner, partly as atonement and partly because she was reluctant to disturb the baby who'd fallen asleep against her shoulder. Holding him so long was an enjoyable novelty, his breath coming in soft puffs against her neck. When her own girls were babies, Megan had felt like a one-woman assembly line. Just as she got one of the triplets to doze off, another would need a diaper or bottle.

Will stood, picking up his plate as well as Iris's empty one. He nodded toward Tommy before carrying the dishes to the sink. "The last thing I want to do is wake him and set him off again, but if I let him sleep now, what are the odds he'll sleep for me tonight?" He paused, his expression alarmed. "Do five- or six-month-olds even sleep through the night?"

"They can." At least, Megan thought so. The first year had been a blur. Her daughters had kept her so busy she'd barely had time to be heartbroken over the divorce. In retrospect, she could find blessings in the chaos. "But it's hard to gauge how he'll react to being in a strange place. Did the notebook say anything about his sleep schedule?" Midway through giving Tommy his bottle, Megan had asked Will to look in the duffel bag for a burp cloth. He'd found a tiny spiral notebook with information like the pediatrician's phone number and feeding instructions.

"Not that I saw, but I need to read through it more closely." He returned to the table, pausing by Daisy and raising his eyebrows in Megan's direction.

Megan sighed. "Are you going to eat any more food?"

Daisy shook her head, her dark curls swishing. "Full."

"I shouldn't have given you that chocolate this afternoon."

"Amy mentioned you were giving out chocolate," Will said, reaching for Daisy's dishes.

"It was originally intended for you." Megan squirmed in her chair, fighting the urge to duck her gaze like a guilty child. "As a peace offering for how short-tempered I was last night."

The corner of his mouth lifted in a rueful grin. "I wasn't exactly on my best behavior, either. What do you say, neighbor? Fresh start?"

"I'd like that." Especially since he was helping to clean her kitchen. That was more than fair compensation for her giving the baby a bottle and getting to snuggle him all through dinner. But since Lily would freak out if the tall, broad-shouldered man got too close, it was time for Megan to pitch in clearing the table. "All done?" she asked her daughter.

Lily nodded. She'd barely taken a bite, too busy watching their guest with a mixture of fascination and anxiety. Megan would put the kids' leftovers in the fridge for lunch tomorrow. Cradling the baby against her with one hand, she took Lily's plate and crossed the kitchen. Looking into the adjacent living room, at pint-size furniture and toys strewn across the carpet, she tried to think of anything the girls had outgrown that she could lend Will for the next couple of…days? Weeks? He hadn't said when Amy was coming back, or why she had chosen him as Tommy's caregiver in the meantime, and Megan hadn't pressed for details in front of her daughters.

"Since you girls are all done eating, how about we put in that DVD we checked out from the library?" That would give her a few minutes to talk to Will without an audience. She found herself reluctantly curious about him. The last few months had given her an up close view of his social life, and she'd thought she understood him pretty well. But based on his patience with her daughters, his willingness to pitch in with dinner and the huge favor he was doing for Amy, maybe Megan had judged him too harshly. *Not all men are Spencer.*

True, but she'd been naive about her ex-husband, giving him the benefit of the doubt far more often than he deserved. It was a mistake she wouldn't allow herself to repeat.

She went around the corner to get the DVD started. When she returned to the kitchen, Will was wiping down counters. "Thanks," she said, "but you don't have to do that."

"Yeah, I do. I want to make sure I stay in your good graces for the next time I have a Tommy emergency." He eyed the sleeping baby in her arms. "No matter how peaceful he looks now, I'm sure we'll face plenty of challenges between now and when his mama gets back."

"How long will Amy be gone?"

"I'm not sure."

She recalled the young woman's tear-streaked face. "Is she all right?"

He was slower to answer this time, the words softer. "I'm not sure."

"You're worried about her." She studied his face, noting the concern in his dark blue eyes and feeling guilty for her assumptions about his selfish, carefree bachelor lifestyle.

"Yeah. She... No offense, but I probably shouldn't be discussing the details of her personal life. Not that I know many of them. She and I aren't *nearly* as close as you imagined."

"Close enough that she trusts you with her child." When he stiffened, she clarified, "I meant that as a compliment. I really am sorry I leaped to conclusions."

"I guess, since she left the baby with me, I can understand why you'd think something so far-fetched. It never occurred to me anyone would make that mistake. Most everybody in town knows about her relationship with Donovan." His voice was almost a snarl when he said the other man's name. "I keep forgetting you're new."

She'd moved to Cupid's Bow in January, practically a year ago. In a small town where most of the locals had lived here since birth, she still felt like an outsider. Raising three girls alone didn't leave a lot of time for a thriving social life.

"What made you pick Cupid's Bow?" he asked. "I mean, I love this town, but it's a bit off the beaten path."

"I needed a change after the divorce. I wanted to be someplace…" Where she didn't feel ashamed of her failed marriage and where she wasn't forced to wonder every time she spoke with a female acquaintance, *Did Spencer sleep with you, too?* She shook her head. "Before the girls were born, I worked at a botanical garden. I've always loved plants and flowers. I didn't know Dagmar well before moving here, but she was my dad's cousin. When she decided she wanted to cut back on her hours at the florist shop, she offered me a job. So here I am."

"Just in time to do the arrangements for Cole and Kate's wedding. You know she's from Houston, right? Between the two of you and Sierra Bailey moving here, this is the closest thing to a population boom Cupid's Bow has had since the 1800s."

She laughed at the idea of a three-woman boom, and Tommy twisted in her arms, his eyelids fluttering. "Oops," she whispered.

"Don't worry about waking him. I should get him back to my place anyway."

"Where do you plan for him to sleep tonight? In the car seat? In bed with you?" There was no reason for her cheeks to heat at the mere mention of Will's bed. But now that her attitude toward him had softened, it was a lot harder to ignore how attractive he was. *Get a grip. A hot fireman cleaning your kitchen is no reason to go weak in the knees.* Wait, actually, a hot fireman willing to clean was a pretty solid female fantasy. And here Will was, fantasy made flesh.

In a timely reminder that real life was not fantasy, a rude odor began wafting toward her from the general vicinity of the baby's rear end.

"Amy left some kind of playpen," Will said, seemingly oblivious to the fact that her eyes were starting to water. "I just have to figure out how to assemble it. Then little man can crash in my room with me. I want to be close in case he needs me—not that I'll necessarily know how to help him. I've never even changed a diaper."

She thrust Tommy toward him. "You're in luck."

Will's nose wrinkled. "That does not smell like luck."

WILL COULDN'T REMEMBER the last day he'd had that was so full of surprises. The noxious diaper was an unpleasant surprise; he really could have used a fireman's mask and self-contained oxygen. But Megan finally grinning at him, after months of guarded glances and sharp tones, almost made up for it. As he knelt over the baby, her eyes danced with amusement.

"Good thing I'm a badass with no insecurities," he deadpanned, "or all your laughing at me could be highly damaging to the ego."

Working together, they'd cleaned Tommy up, but

Will had insisted he needed the practice of putting on the new diaper alone. That was proving more difficult than expected. At least the girls had fled the room, protesting the smell. He could just imagine Daisy showing him her properly diapered baby doll and shaking her head at his incompetence.

Now that Tommy was fed and rested, he appeared to think it was playtime. He kept rolling onto his hands and knees, as if to crawl away. Will's challenge was to keep the baby pinned in place without inadvertently hurting him. "I never realized how big my hands are." They looked massive against Tommy's small limbs.

"It can't be that much of a surprise. You're hu…" When she trailed off, he glanced over his shoulder and caught her studying him. "I mean, you're even taller than your brothers."

True. He'd towered over his mother by the time he was in middle school. Did Megan like tall men?

He blinked at the errant thought. *I don't care what kind of man she finds attractive.* Until tonight, they'd barely exchanged a civil word. He sure as hell wouldn't be asking her out.

"Okay." He sat back on his heels. "I think that'll hold. You're free to flip over on your tummy all you want, little man." Tommy did exactly that, pushing himself up onto his hands and knees. He rocked back and forth, not exactly moving forward but gaining impressive momentum. Will watched with concern. "You don't think he can actually crawl, do you?"

Real mobility probably required some kind of baby-proofing. Megan's living room had safety covers in the outlets and gates in the doorways. When she'd unlocked a series of gates for the girls earlier, he was reminded of the weekends he helped on his friend Brody's ranch, herding cows through pens into the chute. But he'd refrained from comparing Megan's daughters to cattle out loud.

She was watching the baby's movements. "Doesn't look like he's crawling yet, but it won't be long. And I warn you, once it happens, they move faster than you'd expect."

Fantastic. *Amy, you'd better get back to Cupid's Bow soon.* More terrifying than anything else—even toxic diapers—was the open-endedness of the situation. He'd been sincere about wanting to help Amy, but he couldn't keep a baby indefinitely.

What were his other options? He couldn't stomach the thought of handing over the infant to Donovan or, after reading Amy's letter, her mother. And calling social services would feel like a total betrayal. So, for now, he'd be patient and take his unexpected guardianship one day at a time.

He lifted Tommy in front of his face. "We've imposed on Ms. Rivers long enough. Think we can manage by ourselves for the rest of the night?"

The baby gurgled happily, blowing a spit bubble.

"I'll take that as hearty agreement."

"Here." Megan reached over to a small table and pulled a crayon out of a basket, then scribbled something across a piece of paper. "In case you have any emergencies tonight."

"Thank you." He stared at the purple digits. Megan Rivers was the last woman in town he ever would have expected to give him her phone number. Although hoping not to need it, as he folded the piece of paper into his pocket, he realized he was surprisingly happy to have it.

Chapter Six

As dawn stretched across the sky and the sunlight spilling through his bedroom window grew brighter, Will knew his chances of getting any decent rest were dwindling. His longest stretch of sleep all night had only been an hour long. It wasn't that Tommy had been unreasonably demanding. He'd only needed one bottle, around four in the morning. Will had stubbed the hell out of his big toe while maneuvering through the dark room for diaper supplies, but the night had been otherwise uneventful. Still, he'd been plagued with uncharacteristic insomnia.

Will had spent plenty of nights on call at the station house; firefighters had to rack out and grab sleep whenever they could. But having a baby in his care was unlike anything he'd ever experienced. It made him feel both fiercely protective and uneasy. His senses had been on high alert as he listened to the baby's every shift and sigh, adrenaline surging each time he thought Tommy was about to wake. Meanwhile, Will's overtired thoughts had returned to Megan Rivers again and again.

Will had periodically complained to buddies about Megan's surly nature, but perhaps he'd misjudged her.

We misjudged each other. Now that he had a better idea of how challenging it could be to take care of one child, he marveled at her ability to raise *three* alone. She'd mentioned a divorce last night, and he idly wondered about her ex-husband. Will's parents had tried to teach their sons that family was sacred. Had Megan's husband fought to hold on to his wife and children? Did her ex do anything to help her parent? Will couldn't recall a man visiting next door.

Then again, you've been busy with your own social life.

It occurred to him he might need to cancel some plans, like his date for the movies with Leanne on Tuesday. This evening, he was attending the town square Christmas tree lighting ceremony with his family; he'd told Anita Drake that if they ran into each other, they should grab dinner at a new restaurant he'd been wanting to try. *I wonder if Anita likes babies.* Regardless, he certainly wouldn't be having any overnight guests while Tommy was here.

He turned his head toward the crib, glancing down at the reason his love life was on hiatus. Tommy slept on his front, knees scrunched up beneath him with his butt in the air. Since there were currently no odors coming from that direction, Will could appreciate that the baby looked kind of cute. His face was to the side, his cheeks round and squishy.

What is wrong with you? He had no idea how long this peace and quiet would last, but instead of making coffee, he was grinning over a baby's "squish" factor? Insane. He swung his feet to the floor, moving as silently as possible. He hadn't been so afraid a mattress would squeak since sneaking Tasha into his bedroom when they were high school seniors.

He tiptoed into the kitchen, brewing coffee and pulling out ingredients for breakfast while straining to listen for any movement from Tommy. Maybe he needed to get one of those baby monitors like the one Megan had carried when she'd stormed over here Friday night. *Megan, again.* He shook his head briskly, as if he could dislodge thoughts of her.

The phone rang on the kitchen counter, and he dove for it before it could ring again, potentially disturbing Tommy. "Hello?"

"Good morning, William. Hope I didn't wake you," his mother said. "You keep such unpredictable hours." Occasionally, he worked strings of double shifts. It meant late nights, but then allowed him three or four days off in a row. "And I never know if you're...um, entertaining."

His mother wasn't as approving as his father about Will's dating habits, but since she hoped he would find someone to settle down with, she didn't lecture him. Mostly, she pretended his sex life didn't exist, which, as far as Will was concerned, was what all parents and grown children should do.

Actually, Mom, I'm not alone. What was the best way to tell her about his new roommate?

"Anyway." She cleared her throat. "I noticed you tried to call me yesterday. Everything okay?"

Not exactly, but breakfast should help restore his optimism. In his experience, the world always looked brighter after caffeine and bacon. "There's no reason for you to worry, I promise. But I would like to talk. In person. Could you maybe come by later?"

"Well, now I'm curious. Is this wedding-related?"

"No." Although he might need her help finding a babysitter so that he could fulfill all his best man duties.

"Need suggestions on what to buy for Christmas gifts?"

"No." Would Amy be back by Christmas? As he stirred a spoonful of sugar into his coffee, it occurred to him that maybe he would need to do some Christmas shopping for Tommy. No way could he let the little man's first Christmas pass without any presents.

His mother sighed. "Well, I do. I'm drawing a blank for what to get Kate's son. I want something that says welcome to the family without it seeming like I'm trying too hard. I don't want to make the holiday awkward for him. And what do I know about fourteen-year-old boys?"

"You raised three of them."

"Yes, but I try to repress the memory. Your collective high school years were the most harrowing of my life. Worrying about college admissions, sports injuries, your brother spiking the prom punch... Cole wasn't too bad—although he was the first one to get his license, and I had an anxiety attack every time he drove anywhere—but Jace was always finding new ways to get himself in detention."

"*I* wasn't a troublemaker." He hadn't meant to sound smug, but years of sibling rivalry momentarily eclipsed maturity.

"Maybe not, but you and Tasha were all over each other. I lived in terror that she'd end up pregnant before the two of you graduated."

"Mom!" So much for pretending his sex life didn't exist.

"Never mind. It was insensitive to bring her up. But teenage boys…" She said it with a shudder in her voice.

He quickly changed the subject. "Come have lunch with me after church. I can give you suggestions about gifts for Luke, and we can talk."

They were saying goodbye when a cry came from the bedroom. Will disconnected the phone, hastily snagging a crunchy piece of bacon before hurrying down the hall. By the time he reached his room, Tommy had worked himself up to a full-force wail.

Leaning down to pick him up, Will winced. *Guess it could be worse. At least you're not a teenager.*

"WORK WITH ME, little man. Our goal here is to make a good impression. And to keep you from catching a cold." Will's house was almost forty years old; he loved its character, and the beautiful oak trees in the yard, but it could get drafty in the winter.

With his mother due to arrive soon, Will had the baby in the center of the bed and was attempting to change him into his second outfit of the day. When Will had burped him during his bottle, formula had erupted out of the baby like water gushing from the fire hydrant. Will had successfully replaced the long-sleeved onesie with a dry one and was trying to secure the baby's kicking legs into a pair of cordu-roy pants that snapped up the inside seams. Tommy tried to roll over, his partially fastened pants flapping around like tiny cowboy chaps. Meanwhile, Tommy's flailing atop the soft blanket was creating static electricity. His sandy-colored hair stood straight up.

When the doorbell rang, Will swore. *Oops.* How early did babies start processing language? "Forget you heard that." He scooped up the baby, who protested vocally, and headed for the front door. Earlier, Will had thought it would be better to tell his mother about Tommy in person. Now he regretted that decision and his failure to prepare her. She wasn't expecting to find him holding an angry baby with Albert Einstein's hairdo and only one sock. There had been two earlier; Will had no idea what happened to the other one.

Taking a deep breath, he swung open his front door. "I'll bet you—"

"Oh my God!" Gayle pressed her hand to her heart. "You *did* get some girl pregnant."

"The hell I did!"

Her eyebrows shot skyward, and suddenly he was ten years old, caught roughhousing with his brothers.

"Sorry, ma'am," he mumbled. Shifting the squirming baby against his hip, Will took a step backward. "Why don't you come inside?" Across the street, Abe Martin was wrapping Christmas lights around his mailbox post. The man had turned to wave at them, but Will hoped his neighbor was too far away to have heard Gayle's exclamation.

As Will closed the front door, his mother shrugged out of her coat and hung it on one of the wooden wall pegs. Then she turned toward him. "Let's try this again. Son, you look awful."

Did he? He hadn't given his own appearance much thought. But now that she mentioned it, he hadn't shaved or showered, his eyes were probably red from lack of sleep and there was a damp patch of spewed formula drying on his shirt.

"I'm babysitting," he said inanely. "For a friend, a platonic friend. Do you know Amy Reynolds? She works at the bar with Jace."

Gayle nodded. "And answers the phone at the salon sometimes. She had to quit her cosmetology program when she got pregnant."

"Well, I'm watching her son while she's out of town."

"Why you?"

"Because she left rather suddenly, and Amy didn't feel like she had many alternatives. Not positive ones, anyway." He went into the living room so that he could set Tommy down and let him roll around to his heart's content. "That's part of what I want to discuss with you. You're a force of nature in this town. Maybe when she gets back, you can help her find a better job?"

"I don't know. If this woman is the type of person who leaves her baby on a whim, is she a reliable, diligent worker?"

"Mom, she had her reasons for going. Trust me."

Gayle sat on the couch, silently considering his request. "All right. When your friend gets back to town, tell her to call me. But if you want to help her change her situation, the person you should really win over is Becca Johnston. Talk about a force of nature."

That was putting it mildly. Becca was on the town council and ran everything from the elementary school PTA to the annual Watermelon Festival. Becca was also a divorced woman around his age.

Was his mother, known for her occasional meddling, trying to point him toward a suitable potential match?

"Maybe you can talk to Becca at the tree lighting," she suggested. Then she frowned. "You are still going, aren't you? Do you have a car seat for...?"

"Tommy. And yes, I do." Amy had left the base for it in his driveway before making her surprise departure.

She glanced down to where Tommy had pushed himself onto his hands and knees and was lurching wildly back and forth. "I wouldn't be surprised if he's mobile soon. Are you sure you're up for this?"

"Well, I could use a little help." He cast her the same beseeching look he'd used during childhood to get the occasional extra cookie.

But she only laughed. "Don't look at me. Between your brother's wedding, Christmas and three different charity events, I've never been busier. Although I suppose I can stay with him while you go take a shower."

He'd take what he could get. "I appreciate that."

She wrinkled her nose. "So will everyone who has to be around you at the ceremony tonight."

ONE HAND BRACED against a picnic table, Jace doubled over in hoots of laughter, unconcerned with the curious stares of nearby townspeople. "And of all the possible citizens of Cupid's Bow, she picked *you* to babysit?"

Will glared at his brother. "You were the one who told me to call her in the first place."

At that, Jace straightened. "Can I get anyone some hot cocoa? Kate? Cole? I'm feeling the need for a strategic exit."

"Extra marshmallows for me, please," Kate said. "Although, I suppose I'll have to pass this sweetie pie to someone else if I'm going to be holding a hot beverage."

She'd been cuddling Tommy for the last ten minutes, obviously a natural with babies. Judging from the beatific expression on her face and the adoring way Cole was watching her, Will wouldn't be surprised if the two of them decided to have a child together, adding to their blended family. Currently, Cole's twin girls were in line with their grandparents to meet Santa Claus, while Kate's teenage son was talking to some classmates over by the high-school-sponsored gingerbread scale model of town square.

"Um, Kate? Something you neglected to tell me?" Sierra Bailey approached, hand in hand with Jarrett Ross, one of Will's best friends. Sierra raised an eyebrow as she nodded toward the baby.

"We're helping Will watch Amy Reynolds's son while she visits some family out of town." Kate passed Tommy back to Will so she could turn and hug the pretty redhead. "Did you survive the visit with your parents?" Sierra came from a wealthy Houston family, and they'd just made their first ever trip to Cupid's Bow to meet Jarrett before he accompanied her to her brother's high-society wedding.

"Barely."

Jarrett chuckled. "They weren't terrible. Although they did ask several times if I'd be willing to give up ranching, leave Cupid's Bow forever and find a more lucrative job."

"Total snobs," Sierra said. "How do you not find that terrible?"

"Well, they love you a lot. So we had that in common."

She stretched up on her tiptoes to kiss him. "Thank God you're coming with me to my brother's wedding."

He gave her a mock scowl. "I don't know how I ended up having to wear a suit two weekends in a row." If the former rodeo star ever got married, he'd probably show up at the altar in jeans.

Then again, Jarrett was crazy about Sierra. Assuming she was the bride in question, she might be able to talk him into a tuxedo complete with tails and a top hat. When Sierra had first come to town, Will had flirted with her and taken her dancing once, but he had to admit, she and Jarrett were made for each other.

Sierra gave her cowboy a sympathetic smile. "Yeah, back-to-back weddings are going to be a little crazy." She elbowed Kate. "You couldn't have picked a different time?"

"Blame me for thinking a December wedding would be romantic," Cole said.

"I guess my future sister-in-law had the same idea," Sierra said. "At least I'm not in her bridal party. The bright red bridesmaid dresses she picked would clash." She pointed to her auburn hair.

"Nah." Jarrett smoothed a strand away from her face. "You'd just end up rocking the look."

"I would, wouldn't I?" She grinned happily, and then her gaze caught on something beyond him. "Uh-oh. Looks like Megan Rivers and her girls are here. Will, do you need me to cause a distraction while you go hide from the scary florist?"

He turned in the direction she was looking. Sure enough, there was Megan, in a leather jacket and a light blue scarf the color of her eyes. She was carrying one of the girls while the other two toddled along in candy-cane-striped leggings and puffy jackets. He would bet that the one clutching the leg of Megan's jeans was Lily and the one a step ahead of her was Daisy.

"I've never understood why you don't like her," Cole said reproachfully.

"Will told me once that she almost beat him up with a parenting magazine," Jarrett said. "Of course, he also said she moved here a few years ago when he obviously meant a few months ago, so he's an unreliable source."

"I didn't say I didn't like her," Will defended himself. "It was the other way around. And I certainly never said I was scared of her! At any rate, that's all behind us. She's realized I'm a great guy. In fact, I should go say hi." He found himself suddenly eager to talk to her. He wanted to thank her again for her help last night. Even more, recalling the humor lighting her face as she'd laughed at his diapering attempts, he wanted to make her smile again.

Will turn to Cole. "Can you hold Tommy for a few minutes?"

Kate murmured to her fiancé, "A man with a baby is *so* attractive."

Cole stretched out his arms. "I can hold him as long as you need me to."

Will made sure the baby was snugly wrapped in his blanket as he passed him over and that his knit hat was keeping his ears warm. Jace had gotten his wish with regards to the weather—it was the chilliest night so far this winter. The cocoa and hot cider vendors were doing a thriving business as the townspeople waited for the tree lighting, which would happen in another ten minutes after a brief performance of Christmas carols by a local church choir and the high school orchestra.

Barely feeling the cold, Will crossed the square toward Megan and her girls. "Evening, ladies. You arrived at the perfect time—early enough to hear the live music without having a long enough wait for anyone to get bored."

Megan tilted her head. "How do you know we just got here?"

"I…may have been subconsciously watching for you." If Sierra hadn't pointed out the Rivers family, he would have spotted them soon enough. Several times throughout the night, while casually scanning the crowd, he'd felt a leap of anticipation when his gaze landed on a brunette. He could no longer pretend he hadn't been watching specifically for Megan.

"You were?" Her voice was soft and breathy, completely unlike the tone she'd used when she chided him over his car alarm.

"Of course. I needed to find you and thank you for last night."

"You already thanked me."

"That diaper you helped me with—well, really more of a natural disaster than diaper—deserves a million thanks. So be warned, you still have hundreds of thousands coming."

When Megan laughed, Iris craned her head, looking between her mother and Will. "What's funny?"

He shook his head at the girl. "I was just being silly. Are you still excited about seeing Santa, Iris?"

While Iris nodded enthusiastically, Megan regarded him with surprise. "You can tell the girls apart? Most people can't."

"They may be identical, but there are telltale differences if you pay attention. For instance, Daisy is the most talkative." Even as he made the observation, he realized Daisy hadn't said a word since he walked up to them.

Megan glanced down, a frown creasing her forehead as if she was noticing the same thing. "Oh boy," she said under her breath. "I learned early with this one that it's never a good sign when she's quiet." She knelt to set Iris down, then turned to Daisy. "Is everything okay?"

"Uh-huh." But her voice was weak, hardly convincing.

Megan cupped the little girl's cheeks, peering at her face. "Oh my gosh, you're burning up, baby."

Daisy didn't respond, as if she'd barely heard her mother's announcement. Studying her more closely, Will saw that her expression looked glazed. "Is she okay?" It felt disturbingly wrong for the spirited, bossy preschooler to be so subdued.

Megan straightened. "She should be fine, but she's definitely got a fever. I guess it was wishful thinking that nobody else would get sick after Iris's stomach bug the other night."

Hearing her name, Iris stopped whispering with Lily on the sidewalk and turned back toward her mother, just in time to hear Megan say, "I need to get her home right away."

"No home!" Iris wailed. "Want to see Santa!" She threw herself onto the sidewalk while Lily watched, her own bottom lip trembling.

Last night, Megan had saved his ass. The least he could do was try to return the favor. He leaned close, close enough to register the warmth of her body and the faintly vanilla scent of her, and offered in a discreet whisper, "If you and Daisy need to leave, I could bring the other girls home after they see the Big Guy."

Megan's eyes rounded, and for a second she seemed too surprised to speak. "That is so kind of you. But I really can't reward Iris's behavior," she said, wincing at her daughter's escalating tantrum. "And Lily wouldn't want to stay with you. No offense."

"None taken." He grinned. "I recently learned that some females are actually immune to my charm. Go figure."

She returned his smile, but only for a moment before casting another worried glance at Daisy. "Anyway, if her sisters stayed without her, Daisy would be upset tomorrow about missing out. The timing's unfortunate, but we'll have other opportunities this month to meet Mr. Claus. And this way," she added under her breath, "I have a chance to talk them into less extravagant gifts first."

"Then can I help you get the girls to your van?"

There was no parking in the square itself, which meant she had to be at least a street or two away. She had picked up Daisy, who was looking paler by the moment, except for her flushed cheeks. There was no way Megan could also carry Iris, who was now in full meltdown.

"If you start walking," he said, "Lily will follow, right?"

She nodded. "But Iris—"

"I've got it under control," he said, hoping he was right. He was well-known in town, and the spectacle of carrying a screaming child through the crowd would raise questions. But he'd helped defuse one or two of Jace's tantrums when they were kids, not to mention his more recent experience with Alyssa and Mandy. "I've got nieces."

Looking skeptical, Megan took a few steps forward, shooting frequent glances over her shoulder at Will and Iris.

He dropped to his knees next to the unhappy little girl. "Did you bring Santa the picture you drew of him?"

Seeming surprised that Will had addressed her, Iris stilled for a moment, sniffling. "N-no."

"Because I heard that he likes artwork to hang up at the North Pole. Maybe you can see him on another night and bring him a picture." He lowered his voice to a confidential tone. "If he saw you right now, crying and arguing with your mommy, he might accidentally think you belong on the naughty list."

Iris sucked in a breath.

While he had her attention, he followed up with, "What kind of animal is it that pulls Santa's sleigh? Unicorns? Flying cows?" When Iris giggled, a rush of triumph went through him.

"Reindeer."

"Maybe we can pretend that you're Santa and I'm one of your reindeer, helping you fly to the parking lot. Want to ride on my shoulders?"

She nodded eagerly. Will stood, then lifted her into place while she cheered with delight. The five of them headed farther away from the square. As they walked, Will made Iris laugh by suggesting potential reindeer names.

"There's already a Dasher, Dancer and Prancer. Who could I be? What about...Pizzapants?"

"That's silly!"

"Well, I like silly. I can be Will-Silly the Red-Nosed Reindeer."

Even Lily tittered at that, and Will smiled down at her. "Do you want a turn on my shoulders, too?"

Shaking her head adamantly, she scooted closer to her mom. Moments later, they reached Megan's van while the church choir sang the "Hallelujah Chorus" in the distance.

"That's how I feel about having them all buckled in," Megan said once everyone was in the appropriate car seat and she'd slid the van door shut. "Hallelujah. Thank you."

"Hey, what are neighbors for?" Neighborly. Yeah, that was how he felt toward her. He wasn't staring at her grateful smile with an errant urge to trace his thumb over her bottom lip. And he certainly hadn't stolen any admiring glances at how well her dark jeans fit while he was walking behind her.

She climbed into the van, and he turned back toward the square. By the time he rejoined his family, he'd missed the tree lighting.

Cole handed him the baby, his expression shrewd. "You took an awful long time to tell someone hi."

"One of her girls is coming down with something, so I helped Megan get everyone back to the van."

"Megan the florist from the wedding?" Gayle asked. "Sweet girl. And single. We were just discussing that at the flower shop this week."

Cole laughed. "Uh-oh, Will. Mom has that gleam in her eye."

"Don't even think about it," Will told his mother. "If you're antsy to fix up one of your sons, go harass Jace about *his* love life. I'm not looking to get seriously involved with anyone, much less the mother of triplets."

"Oh, I know," Gayle said reasonably. "Then again, Kate and Cole weren't looking for romantic involvement, either, and, two weeks from today, they'll be newlyweds. Life is full of surprises."

Will nodded toward Tommy. "I have all the surprise I can handle right now, thanks."

"Understood. I'll have to come up with some other young men who might be right for Megan."

Imagining Megan smiling up at some guy at the end of a date the way she'd smiled at Will by her van, he scowled.

"Problem?" his mom asked cheerfully.

Other than a diabolical mother, not yet having child care lined up for Tommy tomorrow and a sudden inconvenient preoccupation with his shapely next-door neighbor? "Not at all."

Chapter Seven

Normally, Will entered the station house through the apparatus bay where the emergency response vehicles were parked. But that hallway would've taken him directly past the captain's office. So instead, he and Tommy used the public entrance in front, by the classrooms. He nearly collided with EMT Kim Jordan as she exited the workout room, her dark skin glistening with sweat and a bottle of water in her hand.

She regarded the car seat he carried with surprise. "I didn't realize it was bring-your-baby-to-work day." She bent forward for a closer look at Tommy. "Well, obviously not *your* baby. He's too cute to be related to you."

"Ha-ha." He was accustomed to Kim's lighthearted heckling. She was known for being calmly efficient at even the toughest accident sites and for keeping the guys' egos in check around the station house. "I'm babysitting for a friend."

"And you thought the fire station was a good place to babysit? Good luck convincing the captain of that. If you were going to get a mascot, maybe you should have gone with the more traditional dalmatian."

"I know the baby can't stay here." Firefighters

didn't go out on dangerous calls every day, but the nature of their job was that they had to be prepared to drop everything and respond—especially during rare cold snaps when people who didn't bother with regular chimney maintenance decided to use the fireplace. "Marie Davenport is coming to pick him up." Marie was a retired 9-1-1 dispatcher and his friend Brody's aunt. She'd known Will all his life and said she'd be happy to help, except that she couldn't come to get Tommy until after her cardiologist appointment first thing this morning. She also wasn't going to work as a long-term solution, since she was leaving on Wednesday for Louisiana, where her youngest daughter was due to give birth any day.

Given how much Kate had enjoyed snuggling the baby, Will had hoped his future sister-in-law might be able to help while he was on duty. But her day was packed with wedding plans and piano lessons, getting her students prepared for the holiday recital. Gayle had clearly said she was unavailable, and neither of the two women Will had canceled upcoming dates with seemed particularly motivated to do him a favor. This morning, he'd tried to make day-care arrangements, only to be told Tommy could be put on a waiting list, but there were no available openings.

Kim glanced up and down the hallway, her expression furtive. "Can I hold him?"

"Sure." He lowered his voice to match hers. "But what's with the guilty whispering?" He knew why *he* didn't want to draw attention to himself—so that Captain Hooper didn't put him on bathroom cleaning duty for the next six months.

Kim opened the door to one of the empty classrooms and motioned for him to follow. "Not guilty, just... I turned thirty-three last month and it's embarrassing how loudly my biological clock has started to tick."

He unbuckled Tommy from the car seat, holding him while Kim babbled cheerful greetings and played peekaboo with her hands over her eyes. When the baby smiled back at her, Will passed him over.

She continued to make comical faces for Tommy's benefit, cooing in a higher-pitched voice, "You are just the sweetest, aren't you? Yes, you are!" Without altering her tone, she said to Will, "Tell anyone about this, and I'll kick your ass. Yes, I will!"

"Nobody will hear it from me," he promised. Kim taught self-defense classes at the community rec center. It was possible she *could* kick his ass.

She sighed. "I hate to give him back, but I need to hit the shower."

Apparently, Tommy shared her reluctance to part ways, because when she moved toward the door, he let out a squawk of protest. Will's heart thudded. *So much for keeping a low profile.* "None of that, now, little man. We—"

"What in tarnation was that?" came the captain's voice from the hall. "Did I just hear a baby?"

Kim shot a glance over her shoulder, silently mouthed *Good luck* and slipped away.

Seconds later, Captain Hooper poked his bald head into the doorway. "Trent? Explain yourself." The man's forehead furrowed, his eyes nearly disappearing under bushy silver eyebrows.

"Do you remember Amy Reynolds? That apartment fire last summer?" he prompted.

The captain grunted. "You cut a hole in the roof for vertical ventilation. The Reynolds girl baked chocolate chip brownies for the crew the next week. Sweet kid."

"Right. This is her son. Amy had a personal emergency and asked me to watch him."

"Now, see here, Trent—"

"He's not staying. The babysitter will be here to pick him up any minute." At least, he desperately hoped so.

"All right. But, Trent? This better be the one and only time you bring him into my station."

TUESDAY EVENING FOUND Megan on her living room floor, untangling a string of Christmas lights and fighting the urge to swear as her daughters looked on with eager faces. They'd been begging her to put up a Christmas tree, but since Megan hadn't had a chance to buy one yet, she'd hoped to appease them with some decorations from the garage. *Massive fail so far.* The outdoor lights were snarled in impossible coils, the inflatable lawn snowman had a leak in it and one of the resin caroler figurines she'd unpacked was somehow headless. Worst of all, the LED wall art that was supposed to spell out *NOEL* in shimmery lights had a short in it and just kept blinking *NO* when she plugged it in.

Nights like this are why people put rum in their eggnog.

When someone knocked at the front door, she harbored a moment of fleeting, irrational hope that it was a rum delivery service. It was probably Raquel Abernathy, who hadn't been able to make it by the shop before closing to pick up a custom gift basket; Megan had told her she could come to the house as long as she didn't ring the doorbell after the girls' bedtime.

"Just a minute," she called as she boosted herself into a standing position. She cast the lights a final withering glance, attempting to shame them into co-operation.

To her surprise, the person on the other side of the door wasn't Mrs. Abernathy. Instead, Will Trent stood smiling down at her, Tommy nestled in the crook of his arm.

What a difference a few days could make. On Saturday, when she'd opened her door to Will, she'd felt only confusion and disdain. Now, heady warmth coursed through her and she found herself grinning for no apparent reason. The man was like a walking shot of rum.

She leaned against the door frame. "Hey, neighbor. Long time, no see."

"Have I stayed away long enough for you to miss me yet?" His eyes flashed with humor. "Don't answer that, I'm terrible with rejection."

"Probably because you don't have any practice with it." Women told him yes all the time—and she was starting to understand why.

His laugh had an edge to it. "Shows what you know about my life. Haven't you heard? I was rejected by my own bride-to-be the night before our wedding."

Megan blinked, at a loss for words. Will Trent had been engaged? The most socially active bachelor in Cupid's Bow had been willing to settle down? "I, uh… Come on in." She waved him into the house, trying to regain her composure. Finally, she said, "Sorry about your fiancée. That must've been…" Shocking? Devastating? Soul-crushing? "Difficult."

"She broke my heart."

There were moments in Megan's life when she felt as if her understanding of the world had just been knocked sideways—the day when an OB had told her that not only was she finally pregnant, she was carrying triplets, the day she'd learned that Spencer had cheated on her. This was less extreme but still a challenge to wrap her mind around. She'd always assumed that Will did the heart-breaking, not the other way around.

"It was for the best in the long run," he said. "I fell for her when I was a kid and never got to have the normal dating experiences. We might have resented each other when we were older. But I didn't come over here to whine about my past. How are the girls? Is Daisy feeling better?"

From behind the baby gate that separated the living room from the foyer, Daisy called, "Hi, Mr. Will! Come see our Christmas."

He raised an eyebrow. "Are you guys celebrating early?"

"I'm trying to decorate, but I'm afraid I'm going to lose the sun before I get the lights up outside. And the girls are bummed we don't have a tree yet. On the bright side, Daisy is back to her usual energetic self. Lily ran a low fever yesterday and didn't have much of an appetite, but everyone seems fine now. Fingers crossed."

"Good. So now for my other, more selfish reason for coming over. It has been pointed out to me that, no matter how cute Tommy would be in a miniature firefighter outfit, he can't hang out at the station while I work." He held up his free hand as if trying to ward off any argument before she made it. "I know you have a busy work schedule, too, but you're usually home by early afternoon, right?"

"Well, yes. But—"

"Because Kate and her grandmother can help me out most mornings. It's the afternoons that get trickier with Kate teaching piano lessons. And I thought, with Christmas right around the corner, you might be able to use the extra income from watching Tommy."

He had her there. The problem with three children dictating letters to Santa was that there was no sane way to explain why a man gifted with magical elves and flying reindeer would be limited by something so mundane as a budget.

She bit her lip, weighing the extra cash against the extra work. "I don't know."

"You don't have to answer yet." He tried to look innocent. "Why don't you think about it while I hang up these lights for you?"

"You mean, while you leave me with the cute baby in the hopes he'll win me over?"

Will grinned shamelessly, handing her Tommy. "Any chance that might work?"

Hell, she'd probably agree to his child-care proposition just to get assistance with the stupid Christmas lights. It felt like forever since she'd enjoyed the luxury of someone else's help. Since the divorce, she'd shouldered so much alone. It had caught her off guard Sunday when Will offered to do the favor of taking Lily and Iris to see Santa. Even though she hadn't taken him up on it, she'd been genuinely touched by the suggestion and found herself frequently smiling over the last two days at the memory of how he'd carried Iris on his shoulders and made her laugh.

She pointed toward the living room. "The lights are in there. But we have to get them untangled and find which bulb is out before we can hang them up."

"On it." He strode in that direction, exchanging greetings with the girls. Lily didn't say anything to him, but she didn't shy away when he waved to her, either. That was progress. It had taken her months to really warm up to her day-care teacher.

Will turned the task of unknotting the lights into performance art, entertaining the triplets by pretending it took all his strength to pull the cord free. Megan was surprised to find herself amused by the very chore she'd been silently cursing ten minutes ago. *Life is easier with a partner.*

At times like this, she could understand why her mother had fought against the divorce, believing Megan's life would be simpler if she stayed with Spencer. But there were worse complications than uncooperative Christmas decorations. If Megan had stayed with him after his multiple betrayals, she would've grown to despise them both. She amended her earlier thought. Life wasn't automatically better with a partner, only with the *right* partner. Spencer hadn't been that for her, and it sounded as if Will's ex had proven to be the wrong one for him.

He certainly found a bright side in the breakup. If Will had lacked the "normal" young adult dating experiences, he was more than making up for missed opportunities.

"All right," he said. "Time to go make your house

the envy of the neighborhood. You have tools and a ladder, or should I get mine from next door?"

"In the garage. How about I order a large pizza while you work?" She'd been so preoccupied with decorations that she hadn't given dinner much thought.

"Sounds perfect. But so you know, I don't show up here at suppertime just to mooch free food." He winked at her. "I *also* come to mooch the free child care."

She laughed. "Oh, don't worry, if I take your babysitting job, you'll be getting a bill for my services." And as far as the free pizza went? If he got those blasted lights working, she'd even spring for a side order of cheesy garlic bread. "What do you like?"

A slow grin spread across his face, and for no good reason whatsoever, heat climbed in her cheeks.

She gave him a stern look over the top of the baby's head. "On your pizza, William."

"Anything but mushrooms. But I can pick them off if you want them."

"Actually, I hate mushrooms."

"Common ground, huh? Why, Miss Rivers, this could be the beginning of a beautiful friendship."

ALTHOUGH WILL'S STOMACH rumbled appreciatively at the smell of pizza wafting upward, he told Megan that she and the girls should start without him. "I'm almost finished," he called down to her, trying not to let his gaze linger on the enticing V-neck of her sweater from atop the ladder. Admittedly, she was beautiful, but his phone's contact list held the numbers of a dozen beautiful women. Physical appearance wasn't what made Megan special.

He valued the unexpected, burgeoning friendship between them. Flirtatious banter and easy smiles were second nature to him, but if he crossed a line, would Megan return to her disapproving glances and curt, one-sentence conversations?

The ladder wobbled as he shifted to watch her walk into the house, and he almost rolled his eyes at his own idiocy. Firefighters responded to a wide variety of 9-1-1 calls. How many accidents and home injuries had he seen that were caused by someone not focused on what they were doing? He knew better. Pushing aside thoughts of Megan, more or less, he concentrated on the job at hand.

He might have helped her cross Christmas lights off her to-do list, but from his vantage point, he couldn't help noticing other odd jobs that needed attending. There were some shingles on the roof that needed replacing, the gutters needed to be cleaned out and there was a decrepit tree far too close to the house that should probably be cut down before some spring storm knocked it over. None of which was any of his business, but this was Cupid's Bow. Neighbors looked out for each other.

That's right, keep defaulting to the "neighborly" argument until it starts to feel convincing.

He climbed down from the ladder and plugged in the cord to make sure the lights worked. Perfect. He turned them off, smiling in anticipation of showing the girls, and went inside, where he was greeted by the heavenly scent of sausage and tomato sauce and still-warm-from-the-oven pizza crust.

"Success," he told Megan. "We can have the great unveiling after everyone's finished."

As a firefighter, he helped people daily, in capacities as minor as rescuing cats from trees to literally pulling people out of burning buildings. And yet it was the beaming smile Megan shot him from across the table that made him feel heroic. That kind of reaction could be addictive.

He broke eye contact, clearing his throat. "Where do you, um, keep the glasses?"

"Here." She crossed the kitchen and pulled a tumbler from a cabinet. When she handed it to him, their fingers brushed and he couldn't help wondering—if she hadn't been holding a baby just then, if they didn't have an audience of three little girls, would he have succumbed to the urge to tug her closer? To wrap his hand around hers? Maybe—*don't even think it*—kiss her?

Damn. You thought it.

"Thanks." He jerked away and filled the glass with cold water. "I, uh, noticed while I was out in the yard, there's some other stuff you could probably use a hand with."

Her lips thinned. "Is this like when representatives from the neighborhood show up to say the lawn isn't mowed well enough and I'm dragging down property values?"

"Not at all. No criticism, I promise. But you've already done so much to help me with Tommy, and if you ever need my help… I mean, being on ladders is half my job, so cleaning out your rain gutter would be nothing. And I'm supposed to stay physically active. The county pays for us to have state-of-the-art workout equipment, for pity's sake, and—" When he realized he'd started babbling, he stopped abruptly.

Smooth, Trent. This your first day trying to talk to a woman? "So. Pizza!"

He'd finished one slice and was reaching for another when Megan caught his gaze. "Sorry I got defensive when you commented on the yard. Guess you were right about me the first night you came over," she said. "I can definitely be 'prickly.' Since the divorce, I've worked hard to be self-sufficient. I didn't really have a choice. But somewhere along the way, I may have forgotten how to accept help gracefully."

"No apology necessary. Your yard is none of my business, and my family has a history of overstepping our boundaries. It turned out well for Cole, whose childhood habits of finding facts and being bossy work in the sheriff's office, but for the rest of us..." Would now be the right time to warn her that his meddling, overstepping mother might try to fix Megan up on dates?

"Mr. Will?" Daisy's small face was crinkled with impatience, as if she couldn't understand why no one's attention was on her. "Guess what I saw today? Mr. Abe's dog made a *big* poop on the sidewalk."

"Daisy! That is not appropriate talk for the dinner table," Megan chided.

Will tried hard not to undermine her authority by laughing out loud. "I grew up with two brothers," he reassured Megan softly. "I'm not easily grossed out."

"Still." She shot one last stern look at the irrepressible Daisy. "I think a change of subject is in order."

"Are you busy Thursday evening?" he asked. "Because, as it happens, I don't have a Christmas tree, either. We could go shopping together."

"Seriously?"

"Sure. Why not?"

"The girls are liable to be…excited. To put it mildly. Not everyone wants that kind of chaos taking up their free time."

The invitation had been sheer impulse, one he didn't want to examine too closely. So he nodded toward Tommy, his tone nonchalant. "Until Amy gets back, my time's not free anyway. Why not spend it with four lovely ladies, who I'm willing to bet have excellent taste in Christmas trees?"

Daisy and Iris excitedly chanted, "Christmas tree! Christmas tree!" Lily grinned, her round cheeks covered in tomato sauce.

Megan smiled fondly at them and then turned back to Will. "Looks like you've got yourself a date."

"Excellent. Now, who wants to go outside and see the lights?" he asked.

"First, you have to wash hands and faces," Megan said over her daughters' delighted squeals. They scampered out of the room in a rush of footsteps that were surprisingly heavy for such little girls.

Will laughed. "Would you be offended if I said I'd witnessed cattle stampedes that were quieter?"

"See what I mean about the chaos?"

"I don't mind." His own childhood had been full of stomping feet and muddy boots.

"Then you're a better man than their father." Immediately, she straightened in her chair, her expression appalled. "I didn't mean to say that. It's just, Spencer will be here in two weeks, and part of me is dreading it. The girls need a father, so I'm glad he's coming, but his visits are always so strained. He spends his time in the grown-up world, golfing at country clubs or wining and dining clients. He's palpably uncomfortable around sticky hands and occasional tantrums."

"Is that why you two divorced?" Will asked, filled with an extreme dislike for the unseen Spencer.

"I—"

"Mommy! All clean!" The triplets raced into the room, their socks skidding a little on the tile floor. Will stood, planning to intervene if it looked like anyone was going to crash into the kitchen island.

Megan rose, too, instructing the girls to grab their shoes and coats. Then they all tromped outside. Will took the baby so that Megan could have the honor of plugging in the display. He couldn't help chuckling at the heartfelt oohs and aahs, which would have been more suited to the aurora borealis than a few measly strands of multicolored lights.

"If you guys want to see something really impressive," he said to Megan, "go by Brody Davenport's ranch this month. They do an annual light display to raise money for the hospital's children's center. We're setting up this Saturday, and it covers a hundred acres. Admission is whatever small donation visitors choose to make, and Brody gives it all to the center."

"I'll definitely put that on my calendar, thanks. Do you have someone to watch Tommy while you're helping with that Saturday?" At his nod, she said, "As for someone to watch him while you're at work, I've decided I can use the cash. So you're covered, as long as we can make our work schedules match up."

Relief washed over him. He'd known when he picked up Tommy at Marie's earlier that he was running out of options. "I'll trade some shifts if necessary. Thank you so much." Despite how glad he was to have found a solution, his conscience demanded he ask, "Are you sure this won't cause too much trouble for you?"

"It could make things a bit more hectic, but hectic is where I live." She shrugged, giving an endearingly lopsided smile. "Might as well embrace it."

Too bad her husband hadn't been able to do that. It was a shame her marriage had ended. She talked about the girls needing a father, but what about her? Did she ever want a husband to hold her hand and brave the chaos with her? To tease her until her harried expression melted into that sweet smile? To take the garbage to the curb for her after she'd had a punishingly long day or carry a Christmas tree into the house? Will's mother was right—Megan deserved a good man.

In the meantime, she's got me.

Chapter Eight

Like most of the other admittedly biased citizens of Cupid's Bow, Will believed that the Smoky Pig had the best barbecue in the state of Texas. The tantalizing scent that greeted him as he walked into the restaurant nearly made him groan in pleasure.

"Will!" Leanne Lanier set a couple of iced teas down on a table in the corner and hurried toward him. "It's a relief to finally see you, sugar. My sister almost had me convinced I was getting the patented William Trent brush-off, but she's always had an overactive imagination."

"William Trent brush-off?"

"Never mind that, now that you've come to see me."

He experienced a small but sharp bite of guilt, like a paper cut. When he'd told her they needed to reschedule their movie date, it probably would have been more honest to say they needed to postpone indefinitely. But since he'd had no idea how long Tommy would be staying with him, he'd opted for vagueness. "It's always nice to see you. But I'm actually here to pick up a to-go order."

Leanne pouted. "You'd rather go home and eat

dinner all by your lonesome than sit in my section? Or…will you not be alone?"

"As a matter of fact, I won't be. There will be five of us, plus the baby."

Her eyebrows rose. "You mean you're still baby-sitting for that friend you mentioned?"

"Yeah. The woman who lives next door to me lends a hand while I'm at the station. In return, I'm taking dinner to her and her daughters and helping them with their Christmas tree."

"That's right neighborly of you."

Neighborly. He tried not to grimace at the word.

"Hey, Leanne," a customer called, "when you get a chance, we could use refills back here."

She nodded over her shoulder, then said to Will, "Don't be a stranger. I'd hate to tell my sister she was right about that brush-off."

Will didn't know what to say, but he wouldn't make false promises. His enthusiasm for taking her out had waned inexplicably in the last week. "Leanne, I…"

"Damn. I guess even my sister's crazy imagination gets something right once in a while." She put a hand on her hip. "At least tell me I'm still your favorite waitress?"

"Unquestionably. Next time I come in, I'll leave the tip to prove it."

"You'd better," she said as she spun away.

Relieved that there were no hard feelings between them, he resumed his path to the take-out counter. "Order for Trent," he said to the cashier.

Will paid and was gathering the bags when the phone in his pocket rang. No doubt his mother. She'd called twice today about the tuxedo fitting with his brothers tomorrow, then texted him on top of that to remind him he needed to wear his dress shoes for the fitting. *Not my first rodeo, Mom.* The closer they got to the wedding, the more manic she became. Gayle Trent was usually the picture of composure. He couldn't help wondering if she'd become a touch superstitious, after Cole's divorce and Will's abruptly canceled nuptials, about everything going exactly right this time.

Holding his phone between his ear and shoulder, he unlocked the car door. "Hello."

Instead of his mother's purposeful "William..." as she launched into her latest set of instructions, there was a long pause.

"Hello?" He stared at the screen to make sure the call was connected, noting that the unknown number was outside the Cupid's Bow area code.

"Will? It's Amy."

He had a dozen things he wanted to say to her all at once, and he closed his eyes briefly, counting to five so that he didn't demand to know what the hell she'd been thinking. If she'd told Will how desperate the situation was, he could've helped without the last-minute scramble for child care. She should have been honest with him.

"Is..." Her voice trembled with emotion. "Is Tommy okay?"

Her worry for her son dissolved his momentary flare of temper. "He's fine. I'm sure he misses you, God knows I'm no substitute, but he's healthy and well cared for. How are *you*?"

"Better. Shaky. Scared you hate me for what I did.

I was sleep deprived and not even close to being in my right mind."

"I don't hate you."

"Thank you. The counselor here is wonderful. She's helped a lot, but I didn't think I could make any more progress without talking to you first. I needed to check on my boy, and I needed to tell you I'm sorry for how I left him. I knew he'd be safe with you, but I was afraid that if I asked you outright, you'd say no."

Would Will have refused? He had genuinely wanted to help, but taking care of the baby was so daunting. It took him, Megan *and* Kate, with occasional assistance from others, just to make sure Tommy was covered around the clock. He was starting to understand how overwhelmed Amy must have felt. "When you come home, my mom wants to talk to you about possibly finding a better job so that you can cut back on your hours. And, just so you know, my soon-to-be sister-in-law completely adores your son, so maybe she can periodically lend a hand instead of your mother."

Amy sniffled. "I don't know what I did to deserve you in my life. You're like a guardian angel."

"Let's not go overboard, kiddo. I'm no angel."

"Are you with Tommy? Could you hold the phone up to him so he can hear my voice?"

He hated to disappoint her. "Sorry, he's with Megan—you remember the nice lady who gave you the chocolate? She watches him sometimes while I work."

"Oh."

"Maybe you could call again sometime soon?" Or, even better, come see him in person. Trying not to

sound too impatient—her recovery was important—
he asked, "When are you coming home?"

"I… It's difficult to tell. The counselors say that
if you leave too soon, you'll almost certainly relapse.
As much as it kills me to be away from him, I have
to do what's best for him in the long run."

Will's neck and shoulders stiffened, tension radi-
ating to the base of his skull. "Okay. So, what are we
talking here? Days? Weeks?" He almost choked on
the word. He hadn't even made it through one full
week, and it felt as if Tommy had turned his life up-
side down. Plus, he had best man duties and Christmas just around the corner.

"I have to go," Amy said in a rush. "Give him
kisses for me, and don't forget his well-baby appointment on Monday."

"Well-baby?"

"At noon. It's in the notebook."

"Amy, wait! What if—"

"God bless you, Will. You truly are a hero."

Then she hung up, and he sat alone in his car,
swearing heroically.

MEGAN OPENED HER front door, feeling a moment of
surreal intimacy as she situated the baby against her
hip and smiled up at Will, half expecting him to say
"Honey, I'm home." It was like misplaced déjà vu, as
if it should remind her of her marriage, except that
her marriage had been nothing like that after the girls
were born. When Spencer had returned from business trips, there were strained silences and unspoken
suspicions, not smiling reunions.

Will held up two plastic bags. "I come bearing barbecue."

"My hero." It had been a long week and when he'd called to tell her he could take care of dinner, she'd nearly wept with relief at the idea of not cooking.

His face crinkled in an unreadable expression as he took Tommy, who'd reached for Will as soon as he walked inside.

"What is it?" Megan asked.

"You're the second woman to call me a hero today."

Not surprising, given his career. "Did you put out a fire? Save a cat from a tree?"

"It wasn't work-related. I heard from Amy."

"How is she?" Although Megan still didn't know the exact details of where the young woman had gone or why, she'd started listening more closely to local gossip whenever Amy or Donovan was mentioned and she had some educated guesses.

"Better, I think. But she's not sure when she'll be back." He sounded as if he was trying to keep irritation out of his voice.

She mentally applauded the effort even as she sympathized with how hard this must be for him. Before the girls were born, Megan had read stacks of books, taken classes and even printed out internet articles on parenting, yet once the triplets came, there had been dozens of days when she felt unprepared and overwhelmed. Will, in contrast, hadn't been given much notice before a baby was dumped in his lap, disrupting his bachelor lifestyle.

"I like the little guy," he was quick to add. "But not knowing how long he'll be with me or what kind of plans I should be making…"

"I understand." She reached out and squeezed his hand. "For what it's worth, I think you're handling it like a champ."

He glanced down to her fingers over his, and when he raised his gaze again, his expression had changed. Heated. A twinge unlike anything Megan had experienced in years fluttered in her midsection. *Oh boy.* She dropped her hand, but that quivery feeling inside her didn't go away.

Knowing her cheeks were growing red, she quickly turned toward the kitchen. "This smells so delicious I don't even care that my daughters are going to have barbecue sauce all over them in ten minutes. Girls, dinner!" Yesterday, as soon as Will had arrived to pick up Tommy, Daisy and Iris had clustered in the doorway, both clamoring to tell him about their day. Luckily, yesterday's recap had not included any mention of Abe Martin's dog.

She knew that the only reason the girls hadn't come running when Will knocked on the door this evening was that they were finishing up their pictures. When she'd reminded them earlier to be sure to thank Will for coming with them, Iris had wanted to express her gratitude with a drawing. The other two had liked this idea, especially Lily, since drawing didn't actually involve speaking to anyone.

They all gathered at the table. For a change, Megan didn't have to ask anyone to quit playing with their food—or, in Daisy's case, remind her to stop talking long enough to eat something. The girls ate quickly, either in testament to how good the food from the Smoky Pig was or in excitement for their outing. Iris finished first and bolted from her chair. Moments later, she reappeared in her chunky winter coat, her gloves on the wrong hands and dragging her scarf behind her.

"Zip me, Mommy?"

Megan bit her lip to keep from laughing. "Oh, honey, it's not cold today. Don't you remember? You said you were hot when we went to see Miss Hadley at the library."

Iris thrust out her bottom lip. "But Christmas trees!"

It probably didn't help that, for the last two nights, Iris's requested bedtime story had been a picture book about a little girl and her father tromping out in the snow to look for the perfect Christmas tree. "The irony," Megan told Will, "is that if it were freezing outside, it would take us forty-five minutes to locate both of her gloves." She shrugged. "Okay, Iris. You can always take off the coat if you get too warm." Megan was bringing the megastroller anyway, since Will didn't have one for the baby. They could throw Iris's extra clothes in it when she began shedding them.

All three girls got ready with impressive speed, and even Tommy seemed swept up in the enthusiasm, vocalizing lots of *mmm* and *g-g-g* sounds. While Daisy tried to make a run for the door in mismatched shoes, Lily hung back, tugging on the hem of Megan's boat-necked T-shirt.

"What is it, honey?"

"Mis-tah Will's dwawing," the girl whispered. She made a beeline for the living room and returned with all three slightly crumpled drawings, which she thrust at her mother.

"Wouldn't you rather give them to him yourself?"

Megan prodded. There was a fine parenting line between nudging your child out of her natural comfort zone and supporting her sense of security. When Lily shook her head, Megan sighed. "Will? The girls made these for you. To say thanks for coming with us tonight."

"Thank you, Mr. Will," Daisy and Iris chorused.

He looked startled by the outpouring of gratitude, maybe even a little uncomfortable. But then he knelt down so that he could study the pictures at the girls' eye level. He gave each sheet of paper serious study, as if he were admiring museum paintings, and Megan swallowed, her chest tight. The girls had a fairly limited social circle—their mama, the people from day care, librarian Hadley Lanier, their "aunt" Dagmar. Watching this big man patiently make the effort to fit into their three-year-old world took her breath away.

"...and these are all the forest animals with their Christmas tree," Daisy said, pointing to each one. "Bunny. Fox. T. rex."

Will smothered a laugh, his eyes dancing. "This is, hands down, the very best Christmas drawing with a dinosaur in it I've ever been given. Thank you, darlin'."

"And this is *my* picture," Iris interrupted. "See all the snow? Christmas is s'posed to have snow."

Smoothing out the final sheet, Will glanced at Lily. "And you drew this one?"

She nodded.

"It's beautiful." The paper was dominated by a triangle-shaped blob of dark green with different colors decorating it. "A perfect Christmas tree."

Lily's smile was tentative, but she stood taller.

"Well, ladies." He held up the tree drawing. "This is our mission. Let's go find the perfect tree!"

Daisy let out a whoop of glee as Will opened the front door for her. There was a flurry of activity as the girls climbed into their booster seats and Will strapped Tommy safely into his infant seat. He paused by the passenger door, laughing.

"What's so funny?"

"I'm about to get in a minivan." Will shook his head in amusement. "With four car seats. And a triple stroller. My reputation may never recover."

The giddy glow that had enveloped her as she watched Will discuss the drawings with her daughters dimmed. She knew he was kidding around, not taking jabs at her lack of cool, but his joke highlighted the differences in their situations. What had he said earlier this week? *Until Amy gets back, my time's not free.* But Amy *was* coming back. This wasn't his real life. He would go back to late nights and serial dating, and Megan would still be driving a minivan with a ginormous stroller in the back.

This is my reality. He's just visiting.

She started the van and popped in a CD of Christmas music, hoping it would cover her suddenly pensive mood.

As they rolled up to the tree farm, she asked, "Are you sure we'll be able to strap both trees on to the van?" They were supposed to find him a tree, too.

"I'll only get a small one for my place. I don't go all out, because I've never spent a single Christmas at my house. We decorate the station, and my brothers and I help our parents put up the giant family tree. My mother considers it an annual tradition to embarrass us with all the horrible elementary school ornaments we made her and terrible pictures of us as kids. Well, terrible pictures of Jace when he had braces and a regrettable haircut. *I* was always incredibly photogenic."

She laughed out loud. "I believe that."

As they buckled Tommy into the stroller, Will asked, "What do you think I should get little man for Christmas? I'm sure Amy will send presents," he hastily added, "but I feel like he should have plenty to open. It's his first Christmas."

Although she was touched by the sentiment, she couldn't help teasing him. "You do realize *he* won't be opening anything, right? It will be a steady stream of 'oh, what's in this bag, Tommy?' Then you open it for him and coo things like 'look, Tommy, it's a stuffed giraffe, just what you always wanted!'"

"This is your response to my sincere request for help? Sarcastic stuffed giraffe references?" He gave her a stern look. "I expected more from you, Megan."

"Okay, okay. No more terrible hypothetical examples." She mulled it over, thinking back to the girls' first year. Her mother had sent gorgeous but impractical dresses. What Megan had really needed was about a million diapers. "I can give you a list of great baby and toddler books. He's probably getting tired of the two that were in his duffel bag."

"Definitely. Just last night, he complained that the suspense of whether or not the boy finds his green balloon wasn't gripping enough and requested that we move on to George R. R. Martin novels."

"Balloon?" Daisy asked, looking around to see if someone was handing them out.

Will glanced down apologetically. "Sorry. I was only making a joke. But who needs balloons when we have rows and rows of Christmas trees to scope out?"

Rows and rows. Oh, goody. Megan tried not to think about how she'd been up since five thirty in the morning and still had wedding pew bows to work on once she got the girls asleep tonight. *At least I'm wearing my comfortable sneakers.* She dimly recalled that there had been a time in her life when she occasionally left the house in high heels. She was pretty sure none of those shoes had been out of their boxes since she'd moved to Cupid's Bow.

"Can I have a reindeer ride?" Daisy asked.

Will looked around, then turned to Megan, his expression puzzled.

"I think she means on your shoulders," Megan said, fondly recalling how he'd coaxed Iris from her tantrum at the festival.

Daisy nodded. "Iris got a turn. I wanna turn."

"Seems fair," Will agreed. "Hold on a sec." He shrugged out of the flannel plaid shirt he'd worn unbuttoned over a dark T-shirt and tossed it into the stroller on top of the jacket Iris had already discarded. Then, in one fluid motion that made Daisy shriek with delight, he scooped her up and onto his shoulders.

Megan tried—unsuccessfully—not to notice his forearms and the ripple of muscles beneath the thin cotton T. If staying fit was part of his job, the man deserved a raise. She pushed the stroller forward and admonished herself to focus on Christmas trees. *Virginia pine. Fraser fir. Bare-chested Will.*

Her pulse sped up, her skin tingling at the memory of his opening his front door wearing nothing but a towel. She'd been struggling for days not to think about that. But her traitorous mind had other ideas.

After Megan had lived in Cupid's Bow for a few months, Dagmar had tried to set her up on a date or two, insisting, "You may not have the time for a grand romance or the desire to remarry, but a woman still has needs."

"Not currently," Megan had protested. "I don't have enough energy to fuel a sex drive."

That had certainly changed. Her libido had not only reawakened, it was well rested and eager.

"What do you think, Megan?" Will's deep voice was an inviting rumble.

She inhaled sharply, terrified that her barely repressed lust was visible on her face. "A-about?"

"About the tree."

"Right. Of course." She stared at the fir in question, not really seeing it, taking a moment to collect herself and hoping she looked like she was thinking deep tree thoughts. "Do you like it, Lily?"

Her quietest child was sitting in the shade beneath the tree, collecting fallen needles.

"This one!" Iris declared, darting across the aisle. "And this one!" Barreling forward, she'd identified three other contenders by the time Megan caught up to her.

"But which one's your favorite?" Megan asked.

"All of them!"

Behind them, Will laughed. "You're gonna need a bigger van."

"Will Trent?" A woman with high cheekbones and sleek blond hair poked her head out from between a couple of cypress trees, then stepped into the aisle with them. "I thought I heard your…" Her breathy tone had changed to one of confusion as she stared at Daisy atop his shoulders.

Will shifted his weight, looking uncomfortable. "Stefani. Do you, um, know Megan Rivers?"

The woman raked her dark gaze over Megan. "Hi. Stefani Coyle, friend of Will's." She gave him a chiding glance from beneath her lashes. "At least, I *thought* we were friends. What gives, Trent? You don't write, you don't call…"

"Been busy."

"Am I going to have to wait for you to enter another bachelor auction and bid on you just to get some of your time?"

"Sorry, no auctions in my future. It was just that once, for charity."

"Uh-huh." The woman stared at him in bewilderment, obviously trying to understand what he was doing here with three preschoolers, a baby and a frumpy single mom.

At least, Megan felt frumpy in comparison. The blonde had an expensive-looking sweater dress and an impeccable manicure. *Last manicure I had was when the girls and I painted our nails in that bubblegum-scented glitter polish.*

"Can we *go*?" Daisy demanded. "More trees."

Megan knew she should scold her daughter for her rude tone, yet couldn't quite bring herself to do it. Because she was feeling anxious to move on, too.

"More trees," Will agreed. "Merry Christmas, Stefani. Nice seeing you."

The woman laid a hand on his arm. "We should have drinks soon. Catch up."

"I don't know. Like I said, busy time."

"Right." She gave him a tight smile. "Merry Christmas." The inflection she put on the words made it sound as if she'd said something else entirely. Then she shot a final glance in Megan's direction and stalked off.

"Just a hunch," Megan said in the awkward silence that followed, "but I don't think she's going to buy flowers from me anytime soon."

"Sorry about that," Will said. "Stefani…has her qualities."

Megan couldn't help wondering if one of those qualities was that Stefani *also* looked great wearing nothing but a towel.

"Daisy, I'm going to set you down for a minute so you can get a better look at the trees, okay?" He lowered the girl to the ground. Within moments, all three girls were giggling and playing hide-and-seek among the pines.

Will lagged behind with Megan and the stroller. "Just so you know, I never dated Stefani."

Had her jealousy been that evident? Embarrassment made her snap, "You don't owe me any explanations about your love life."

He grinned. "Welcome back, Prickly."

Eyes narrowed, she prepared to blast him. But as soon as she opened her mouth, he gave her such a pointed look she ended up laughing at herself. "Busted. The few times I saw Dagmar as a kid, she called me mouse. Still does—her idea of an endearment. Maybe she should have gone with porcupine."

"Or hedgehog."

"Spiny sea urchin."

He guffawed. "Doesn't exactly roll off the tongue."

"Nicknames aside, I didn't mean to get snippy. But your romantic choices are really none of my business."

"I just felt compelled to let you know she was not among my romantic choices. She broke Jace's heart a couple of years ago, and I wouldn't do that to him. I don't think she's accustomed to being told no."

"A woman that beautiful? I imagine not." When he made a noncommittal noise—as if there could be any doubt about Stefani's appeal—she rolled her eyes. "Oh, come on, most guys would salivate at the chance to go out with a flawless blonde."

He stopped walking. "I'm not most guys."

Very true.

With a grin, he reached out to twine a strand of her hair around his index finger. "And as long as we're on the subject, I'm partial to brunettes."

Her breath caught. The most appealing man in Cupid's Bow—possibly the most appealing man she'd ever met—was flirting with her, and she had no idea what to do. Every feminine instinct in her body told her to flirt back, but she wasn't sure she even remembered how. Besides, her girls were only a few feet away. Granted, they weren't paying much attention to the adults, but Megan was pretty sure they'd notice if their mother suddenly threw her arms around a sexy firefighter and started making out with him. Kids were observant like that.

"Will!" A cheerful female voice broke through Megan's deliberations.

"Anita. Hey." Will's tone was warmer than it had been when he greeted Stefani, but his posture was tense, as if he resented the interruption. He put his hand on Megan's back. "Have you two met? This is my neighbor and good friend Megan Rivers. Megan, Anita Drake."

"Nice to meet you," Anita said, stepping forward to shake Megan's hand. "You're in the flower shop on Main Street, right? I've been meaning to stop in. A Christmas arrangement of roses and carnations would brighten up my grandmother's room at the nursing home." Her gaze trailed down to the stroller, where Tommy was sleeping. "Awww. So, is this little guy the reason we canceled dinner?"

"Um, yeah."

"Well, I can't hold it against him. Who could be mad at that face? When your babysitting gig is over, let me know if you still want to check out the new restaurant." She looked up from the baby, belatedly registering Will's uncomfortable demeanor, and abruptly turned to Megan. "You should join us."

"I should?" Megan hadn't expected to be included on their date.

"Absolutely. Assuming you like Chinese food?"

"I like any food I don't have to cook."

"Great. Just let me know if the two of you find a free night." She nodded toward the nearby triplets. "I'm guessing you have your hands full?"

"I have an entire minivan full. But I'll try to work it in," Megan promised, feeling as if she'd just made a new friend.

Anita spotted one of the lot attendants and waved after him to show him which tree she'd selected, call-

ing to Megan, "I'll be by soon for that flower arrangement!"

As the other woman disappeared over a slight hill,
Megan said, "She seemed—"

"I didn't date her, either," he blurted.

Megan raised an eyebrow.

After a second's reflection, he added candidly,
"We've talked about grabbing a bite a few times, but
our schedules never quite matched up. Our relationship has always been casual but friendly."

"Yeah. You have a lot of friends."

"People are drawn to me. It's my strength of character, generous nature, admirable— This would be
more convincing if I could keep a straight face,
wouldn't it?"

"William, I hate to break it to you, but nothing
was going to make that steaming pile convincing."

He grinned. "Will you at least concede that I'm a
likable guy?"

Pretending she had to think it over first, she finally allowed, "Oh, all right." Truthfully, Will Trent
was dangerously likable. Bordering on irresistible.

And the more time she spent with him, the harder
it was to remember why she should resist the draw.

MEGAN STEPPED INSIDE the renovated barn that served
as a headquarters for the tree farm, ready to pay and
head home. On the plus side, she wouldn't have any
trouble getting the girls to sleep tonight. Iris and Lily
had already crawled into the stroller. Even Daisy's
steps were dragging. But the last hour and a half had
been worth it. After intense deliberation, the girls had

selected a spruce that was currently being strapped to the roof of the van. They'd had so much fun.

And so did I. She snuck a sidelong glance at Will, admiring his profile. He was so—

"Will Trent, as I live and breathe." A petite woman with corkscrew curls stopped in front of them, her hands on her hips and a broad smile on her face. "Never thought I'd see the day you'd be pushing a stroller." She eyed Megan with curiosity. "Hi. Tansy Carmichael."

"Megan Rivers, Will's neighbor."

"Will and I used to play a lot of pool together," Tansy said. "I lost more than a few bets to him." The twinkle in her eyes said that she hadn't minded. "But since it's been months since I've heard from him, I found a new pool partner." She nodded toward a good-looking man with an elaborate tattoo sleeve who was paying for a couple of cups of hot cider. Tansy flashed Will a pointed glance that seemed to say *you missed out, buddy*, but then she smiled at Megan. "Are these your adorable kids?"

"Only the girls. Three is a rewarding challenge, but I'm not sure I could handle four," she admitted.

The man Tansy had indicated joined them, passing her a cinnamon-scented cider. His posture stiffened almost imperceptibly when he noticed that she was talking to Will, but he smiled politely. "Ready to go?"

She nodded. "Nice meeting you, Megan. Goodbye, Will."

As the couple exited, Megan smirked at Will. This time, there was no way he could deny a romantic past.

He folded his arms across his chest. "When you

live your whole life in the same small town, you get to know a lot of people, okay?"

Yeah. Especially the female people. She bit back a chuckle, amused that, for once, he was the one being defensive.

There was a short line to pay for trees. While Megan pulled her wallet out of her purse, Lily suddenly scrambled down from the stroller.

"Puppy!" She raced toward a golden retriever sprawled across a large plaid dog bed in the corner.

When the bearded man behind the cash register saw Megan lunge for her daughter, her eyes wide with alarm, he quickly assured her, "It's okay, ma'am. Buster's as friendly as they come, and he loves children."

Sure enough, the dog's tail started happily thumping when Lily plopped down next to him.

Will shook his head in wonderment. "She may be shy with people, but she's sure not timid around dogs, is she?"

"Nope." Megan watched her daughter fondly. "She adores dogs, always has. I keep trying to teach her, though, that she shouldn't approach them without adult permission. Guess we need to keep working on that."

"Mama? Can I pet the doggy?" Daisy asked the question with an air of self-importance, as if drawing attention to the fact that *she* had followed proper protocol.

Megan gave permission, and within moments, all three of her girls were crowded around the golden retriever, who looked positively thrilled with the attention. She sighed. "I don't know what I'm going to do if the girls ask Santa for a dog. Don't get me wrong, I love animals, but I really do have my hands full. The girls are too young to help much with pet care, and my yard isn't even fenced."

A muffled noise escaped Will, as if he was smothering a laugh.

"What?"

"Nothing, I… It's just, after our first meeting, I half expected you to build a fifteen-foot fence between your house and mine. And possibly add a moat. You really did not like me."

"You were too charming." At his blank look, she tried to explain. "Not quite flirtatious, but almost as if you were trying too hard?" When she'd moved in, he was working long hours at the fire station. She'd overheard plenty of local gossip about him before ever meeting him. They met later, one night when he was enthusiastically kissing a woman goodbye at her car as Megan brought out folded moving boxes to the recycling bin. Will's date had driven away, and he'd walked over to introduce himself. She'd found his over-the-top charm off-putting.

Would her first impression have been different if she hadn't already heard stories, if she hadn't witnessed him getting PG-13 in their shared driveway? "My ex-husband, Spencer, is in sales. Getting people to like him is part of his job. And you…reminded me of him. You don't look anything alike, and you don't even have much in common. But there's a vibe."

"A vibe," he repeated disbelievingly. "You didn't like me because of 'a vibe'?"

"Sorry," she said in a small voice. From his point

of view, she must seem very petty to have convicted him for someone else's crimes.

He sighed. "I guess I didn't help matters. The next few times I saw you, I was determined to get a more positive response. A smile, a laugh, something. I just compounded the problem, didn't I?"

Yes. "That's all behind us." She gave him an earnest look, laying her hand on his forearm as she added in an oh-so-sincere tone, "I find you downright tolerable now!"

"Smart-ass."

She cast a glance toward her girls, even though they were far too interested in the retriever to eavesdrop on boring grown-up conversations. "Language, William."

"Smart-butt."

They were next in line. After they'd each paid for their respective trees, Will pushed the stroller along a side wall, so it wasn't in the walkway. Megan joined him next to a shelf of ornaments.

"Girls," she called, "we need to g—"

"One more minute, Mommy!"

She sighed. "You have one minute to say goodbye."

"If it helps," Will said, "this farm also has berry picking in the spring and a pumpkin patch in the fall. I'm sure they can come back and visit Buster some other time."

"Hey!" The bearded cashier beamed at them, pointing toward the ceiling. "You two are under the mistletoe."

Megan's pulse stuttered and she raised her gaze slowly, as if afraid of what she'd find. Yep. A sprig of mistletoe with a red velvet bow tied around it. Her eyes slid to Will's face. He was looking straight at her, his expression hungry. A hot shiver went through her. *He's going to kiss me.* There was an unnatural stillness about him as he met her gaze, a sense of expectancy as he waited for some sign for her, a silent *yes* or *no*.

Her heart was beating madly now, and her throat had gone dry. Licking her lips, she swayed ever so slightly on her feet. It wasn't a step or even a conscious action, but it brought her closer to him. Taking that as his permission, he cupped her face in his broad, warm hands and leaned down, pausing for the barest second, gaze locked on hers, before their mouths met. It was a light, exploratory kiss, nothing that would scandalize those around them, but it was also the first kiss she'd received in two years. Even more staggering, it was *Will*.

Now that his lips were moving over hers, she realized she'd been waiting for him to do this since that moment among the pine trees when he'd told her he liked brunettes. Perhaps the hunger she thought she'd glimpsed in his gaze was just a reflection of what she herself had been feeling. Sensation coursed through her, almost like adrenaline, leaving her shaky in its aftermath. Part of her wanted to kiss him back from now until the new year. The other part was shocked that she'd done this with her daughters in the same room.

She pulled back, already mentally forming an explanation about mistletoe and Christmas traditions; if that didn't work, she'd distract them with candy canes, to hell with how sticky the inside of her van got. But the triplets were oblivious, all hugging Buster and proclaiming their love for him.

She cleared her throat. "Girls? We, um, need to leave." She was hesitant to look at Will. If he seemed disappointed or unaffected by the kiss, she'd cry. Or possibly throw Christmas ornaments at his head. But if she found desire in his expression, how would she keep herself from melting back into his arms?

"Megan."

Moment of truth. She glanced up, suddenly commiserating with Lily's shyness.

There was need etched in his expression—he *definitely* wasn't unmoved by their kiss—but tenderness, too. He opened his mouth to say something, but it seemed his usual slick charm deserted him. Instead, he gave her a lopsided smile and squeezed her hand. Megan realized she was grinning like a teenage girl with her first crush. She wanted to skip through the parking lot or spin in circles for no reason other than the sheer, dizzy joy of it.

It was ironic—for all that three different females had approached him since he'd set foot on the farm, in that moment, grinning back at Megan, he made her feel like the only woman in the world. Or at least, the only one who mattered.

Chapter Nine

Cupid's Bow only had one men's formal-wear shop, and it had been operating for over thirty years. Every so often, the owners did some minor redecorating to keep up with the times, but as Will stood waiting for the associate to bring him his tuxedo, memories swirled around him like smoke. He'd stood in this exact spot in the days prior to his junior and senior proms, both of which he'd attended with Tasha. And this was where he'd rented the tuxedo for his wedding—not that he'd ever needed to wear it.

With each month that passed, he thought about Tasha less and less. Yet, standing here now, he couldn't suppress a sharp spike of anger. It wasn't that he held any grudge for her breaking off their engagement; if she didn't love him enough to make it work, better to find that out before they exchanged vows. But after all the years they'd had together and everything they'd meant to each other, couldn't she have found a less humiliating way to end their relationship? Even after she'd skipped town, he remained an object of pity and speculation.

But he was here today as Cole's best man. He needed to support his brother, not dwell on past wounds. *Get your game face on*. If Will struggled to make it through a simple tuxedo fitting without brooding, how was he going to handle the wedding day? He truly was happy for Cole and Kate. When he stood in front of their family and friends to give his best man toast next weekend, he wanted them to feel his sincerity, not any lingering bitterness.

To Will's left, Jace slid open a floor-length curtain and emerged from a fitting room. He strutted toward the large mirror on the back wall and smiled at his own reflection. "Bond, James Bond."

Will shook his head. "Dork, major dork."

"You're just jealous *you* don't look this suave."

"Give me a minute," Will said, taking his tux from the returning associate, "and I will." As he changed clothes, he couldn't help wondering if maybe Cole should have asked Jace to be the best man. Will had been the best man in Cole's first wedding…which had ended in divorce. And Cole was the best man on record for Will's wedding that wasn't. *Our history is not auspicious.*

Then again, Will thought, adjusting his bow tie, if Jace were the best man, he'd lose the rings and kidnap Cole to Mexico for some wild bachelor party weekend. Which Cole knew perfectly well.

Will exited the dressing room to await his turn while the tailor circled Jace, checking the fit of the shoulders and the back of the coat. The elderly man tutted to himself as he ran a finger beneath the collar. Cole, meanwhile, had already finished with his own fitting and changed back into his sheriff's uniform. He and Will were both taking their lunch breaks; Jace didn't work until this evening, and their father was running late because of an accident on the other side of town.

Will walked over to where his brother sat. "Not much longer until the big day. Excited?"

"I'd say I was the most excited person in the world, but I think the twins have me beat. They are *ecstatic* that Kate is going to be their mother."

"And how are you and Luke doing with the impending stepson/stepfather situation?" Will asked. The two had gotten off to a rocky start when Cole busted Luke for shoplifting on his very first day in town.

"Luke's a teenage boy, so he plays it a little cooler than my six-year-old daughters, but he's started confiding in me. Asking my opinion on what classes to take next year, asking my advice about girls—"

"Ha. If it's romantic advice he wants, he should come talk to his uncle Will."

"Yeah." Cole's expression turned sly. "I heard new romance was brewing in your life. I thought you didn't want Mom setting you up with Megan Rivers."

"I don't want Mom setting me up with anyone," he said neutrally. "I'm a big boy. I can get my own dates."

"Okay, but you *do* realize that she probably heard about you kissing Megan at the Leonard Tree Farm about five minutes after it happened?"

Will groaned inwardly. As a lifelong resident of Cupid's Bow, he knew how swiftly gossip spread. But he hadn't been thinking about the rumor mill when he'd realized the opportunity he'd been given. He'd only been thinking about the sensual gleam in Megan's eyes as she'd glanced from the mistletoe to him, about the softness of her lips beneath his and the way she'd moved toward him. For all the times he'd teased her about being prickly, she'd been so sweet and eagerly pliant.

Cole whistled low under his breath. "Wow. You're not even here anymore, are you? You're thinking about her."

He let out an exasperated breath. What the hell had happened to his poker face? No wonder his brothers had taken his money last time they played. "There was mistletoe. In the spirit of the holidays, I gave her a friendly kiss. I kiss women semiregularly, Cole. It's not breaking news."

"And do you also hang up Christmas lights for them? And buy barbecue dinners for their families? Abe Martin across the street from Megan plays bridge with Dad. And Leanne Lanier gave Kate an earful when she went in to pick up a rack of ribs last night."

"Damn Cupid's Bow," Will muttered. This town was the original information superhighway.

"So, what's happening between you and Megan?"

If the question had come from Jace, all smirking mockery, Will would have automatically deflected. But this was his big brother and Cole had always been there for him, including drinking with him until dawn the night Tasha broke their engagement. So he said honestly, "I don't know. She's…great."

"No argument here. Kate and I like her more and more each time we deal with her."

But however great Megan might be, the romantic relationships Will favored these days weren't relationships at all. They were fun, consensual flings. Based on her past scathing comments about his love life, he strongly doubted Megan would consider a short-lived affair. But anything more than that between them would be fraught with unwanted complications.

They were next-door neighbors. How uncomfortable would life become after their relationship ended? Every time he went to the mailbox or took out the trash would be a potentially unpleasant encounter. Not to mention the awkwardness of running into each other with new lovers. Proximity was reason enough not to get involved, but her girls were an added factor. He and Megan had been lucky yesterday that the triplets had been distracted, but short of buying them a golden retriever, he couldn't keep them from noticing if he and Megan were in a relationship. The first time his nieces, Alyssa and Mandy, had seen their dad kiss Kate, they'd asked if they were getting a new mommy. If the relationship hadn't worked out, those girls would have been devastated. And Megan's girls were even younger. It would be so difficult to manage their expectations or talk to them about the complexities of adult relationships.

He suddenly realized Cole was watching him intently, the way he might scrutinize a suspect he was about to question. "I spent months trying to get Megan to like me. Now she does, and we're friends. End of story."

Cole hitched one eyebrow in such a sardonic, skeptical expression that Will kinda wanted to punch him. Next to socking his brother, his strongest instinct was to deny, deny, deny. But protesting too much would only convince Cole he was onto something. So Will went with the unpredictable. "Maybe I'll ask her to the wedding."

The surprise that washed over his brother's smug

face was supremely satisfying. But Cole recovered quickly. "Um, she's the florist. She'll already be at the wedding, distributing corsages and making sure the pew bows are right, et cetera."

"Well, this is depressing." Shrugging out of his tuxedo jacket, Jace joined them. "I used to look up to my badass older brothers and now I find you discussing pew bows."

"Wrong," Cole said, "we were discussing Will's date, the woman responsible for said bows."

"This would be the woman you were making out with at Leonard's Tree Farm?" Jace asked.

Will's jaw clenched. "The tailor's ready for me now. It would be rude to keep him waiting." He stepped forward, but unfortunately, both of his stubborn brothers followed. "You two are making a big deal out of nothing. I'm allowed to have a plus-one, which would make the reception much more enjoyable, and it occurred to me that since she'll be there anyway and since we're *friends*, I might as well ask Megan." Going on the offensive, he asked Jace, "And your date would be…?"

His brother glared. "I don't have one. But I could if I wanted to! A family wedding isn't exactly a casual outing, like bowling."

"Which is why I didn't ask anyone, either," Will said. "But since Megan will be there, and I'll be there, we might as well dance together and have a little champagne after the best man duties and the pew bows are all finished. Plus, if I have a decoy date, I don't have to worry about Mom shoving single women at me all night."

Jace looked suddenly horrified. "Oh, hell. I didn't

think about that. I'm going to be unprotected, vulnerable! And the ladies won't be able to resist me in a tux." He nodded at his own reflection. "*This* is the kind of suit I was made for, not red polyester. I'm far too young and sexy to be Santa."

"What are you talking about?" Cole asked. "Did you bring a flask to the fitting?"

Will was starting to wish *he* had.

"The bar is doing a winter wonderland event, and my boss has decided that I should be Santa, so I've rented a Santa suit."

Santa. Will had a sudden recollection of Iris throwing herself down on the sidewalk when she'd realized she was being denied her chance to meet Saint Nick. Her cries had been heartbreaking. "How long do you have this suit for?" He grinned as an idea struck him.

"I need to have it back Sunday morning, why?" Jace's expression turned wary. "Oh, hell. I know that smile. I'm not going to like what you're about to say, am I?"

"Nope. But you're going to agree anyway."

WHEN DAGMAR WALKED into the florist shop at one thirty, holding out a salad from the local deli, Megan suddenly realized how famished she was. She'd been so busy that morning she not only hadn't made time for a snack, but she hadn't even had a spare minute to register she was hungry.

"You are a lifesaver," Megan said.

The short, silver-haired woman grinned. "That's how I feel about you, too, mouse. Being able to sleep until noon is nirvana."

"You don't actually sleep until noon, do you?"

Megan asking, rummaging through the deli bag for a fork and salad dressing.

"Just once. After my girlfriends and I went to a ladies' night in Turtle."

Megan laughed. "I'm not sure how to feel about my sixty-five-year-old honorary aunt out partying while I'm home reading *Goodnight Moon*."

"Maybe you should come with us next time."

"Thanks, but the girls keep me pretty busy in the evenings."

"So I hear," Dagmar said with a cryptic smile. "Busy picking out Christmas trees, right?"

Oh boy. What else had her aunt heard? *Like you don't already know.* Megan should have seen this coming. How many times had she overheard locals having animated conversations about each other's lives right here in this shop or in line at the bank or while waiting for their food at the Smoky Pig lunch counter? It was rarely malicious, just nosy. People in Cupid's Bow considered themselves family and seemed to think they had a right to know what their "relations" were up to at all times.

She decided to brazen it out. "Yep, the tree is at home in its stand. We're planning to decorate it to-night, if you want to help." She forked a piece of tur-key in her salad. A person couldn't be interrogated with food in her mouth. "I'd better hurry up and eat this. I have to deliver flowers to Jasmine Tucker, get Tommy from Kate and pick up the girls."

Dagmar pursed her lips. "Too bad we didn't get more of a chance to talk. But who knows? Maybe I will come by tonight for tree-trimming."

It sounded vaguely like a threat, but Megan could

hardly retract the invitation. Instead, she nodded gamely and hoped that the presence of her daughters would prevent her aunt from getting too personal.

After scarfing down the rest of her salad, she drove by Jasmine's boutique a couple of streets over to deliver the flowers her boyfriend, Brody, had ordered. Then she drove to the church; since Kate had to be in town anyway, they'd agreed to meet there. They parked next to each other, and Tommy stayed asleep as Megan moved his seat from Kate's car to her own van.

"Thank you so much for meeting me here," Megan said, checking her watch. She was actually a few minutes ahead of schedule now. That never happened. "It's been a hectic day and this is a lot more convenient than driving out to your grandmother's farm."

"Tell me about it," Kate said with a laugh. "I lived there for months without resenting the drive, but as the wedding approaches, I can't help thinking about how much closer to town the new house will be." She and Cole had decided not to live in his house while they were engaged, instead choosing to move the whole family into the one they'd had built. Together.

"It won't be long now," Megan said. "I finished the girls' bouquets, by the way." Kate, her matron of honor, Crystal, and bridesmaid, Sierra, would carry a bouquet of fresh flowers, similar in shape but each a different color. But Kate had wanted silk arrangements for her stepdaughters that they could keep as a memento of the day.

Kate's eyes shimmered. "I can't believe I'm this happy. After my husband died, I never thought…" She swallowed hard. "Would you believe I actually fought it at first? I was afraid to be happy again."

"I can understand that." Even in the less drastic case of divorce, you walked away with emotional scars. When your entire life crumbled around you, you developed a new sense of vulnerability, an awareness of how easily joy and stability could be taken away.

Kate sniffed. "Good grief. I'm an emotional mess lately. The last thing I want is streaked mascara and puffy eyes in the wedding pictures. I don't suppose you have a tissue?"

"Of course I do. I travel at all times with tissues, assorted first aid supplies and emergency crackers— so that Iris doesn't waste away." Megan leaned into her van to grab a tissue box. "You've never met a child who can go from perfectly content to faint with hunger so rapidly."

"Ha! You've obviously never fed a teenage boy. Thanks," Kate said, dabbing at her eyes.

"I'll make sure to bring extras to the wedding," Megan promised, "and have them stashed in all kinds of subtle, but accessible places."

"About the wedding… We talked about your staying for the reception. You do know we mean that as a thank-you, not a you-being-on-call-for-centerpiece-emergencies, right? We want you to have fun just like the other guests. Have some champagne, dance with a handsome date."

"Date?"

"Hypothetically," Kate said, her expression innocent.

Megan pressed a palm to her forehead. "Is there

anyone in town who didn't hear about the Christmas tree farm kiss?"

"That's kind of a mouthful. We're calling it the Mistletoe Moment."

"Right." Her sex life now came with catchy, alliterative captions. Determined not to overreact, she told herself that one modest kiss did not equal a sex life. *Maybe not, but it's the closest you've come in years.* She sighed. "I think it's time I wake Tommy up and go collect the girls."

"Meaning you don't want to discuss the Moment?"

"I hate to disappoint you, but there's not much to discuss." At least, Will hadn't seemed to think so. Mere minutes after making her toes curl last night, he'd helped her and the girls to the van, helped set up the tree, then taken Tommy home. There'd been no mention of what had passed between them. Of course, it wasn't as if Megan had addressed the topic, either. Given her rather barren social life since the divorce, a kiss might mean something very different to her than it did to Will. Her hastily formed first impression of him as a womanizing degenerate was wrong, but the whole town knew he wasn't exactly celibate.

She leaned into the car and unbuckled Tommy, speaking softly. "Hey there, buddy. Want to see the girls?" She knew from experience that he often woke up in a mood, and sure enough, his face was already scrunching up into a scowl. He let out a tentative cry, like an opera singer doing warm-up scales before a performance. She patted him on the back, her tone soothing. "Oh, I don't think there's really any need for that, do you? We're all friends here. And friends do not assault friends' eardrums."

Kate chuckled. "He does get cranky when his beauty rest is interrupted, doesn't he? Other than that, he's such a good baby. You don't think all of this is bad for him do you? Being passed around from caregiver to caregiver, all the new environments?"

"It takes a village, right? The important part is that he has responsible, loving people who keep him safe and healthy." From what she'd heard about Donovan Anders, Tommy's biological father might not have accomplished that.

Still, it eased her mind when she walked down the church day-care hall and Tommy gurgled happily when he saw the triplets. Sometimes Daisy startled him with her exuberance, but overall he seemed very fond of the girls. Maybe his current schedule was a little unorthodox, but he didn't seem any worse for the wear. Likewise, the triplets didn't seem to mind sharing their mother's attention and limited time.

With all four children in a good mood, Megan wondered if she'd be pushing her luck by stopping at the grocery store on the way home. She knew lots of other moms with young children used their day-care time to run errands, but that was when she needed to be at the flower shop.

Starting the van, she made her voice as upbeat as possible. "Who wants to help me pick out dinner tonight?"

Unable to resist a request that cheerful sounding, all three girls chorused, "Me!"

"Okay. We'll pop into the supermarket for a few minutes and maybe even see if they have any ice cream on sale." She was able to get one of the huge shopping carts that was shaped like a race car at the end. With Tommy safely buckled in the front, Lily and Iris "driving," Megan only had to contend with Daisy running wild in the aisles. She reviewed her goals—make sure she picked up some green vegetables, get a pack of Christmas cards for the girls to exchange at the preschool party, double-check that Daisy didn't sneak items into the cart and get out of here before anyone had a meltdown.

She headed for produce first, so that they'd end in the frozen section on the other side of the store. No point in her ice cream melting while they shopped. "Okay, do we want bananas for snacks or—"

"Will!" Daisy called, taking off at a dead run. Iris and Lily both poked their heads out either side of the car to take a look. Megan turned to see three firefighters in uniform. Sure enough, Will was one of them.

He was currently high-fiving her daughter. "Guys, this is the wonderful artist I was telling you about. Daisy, I have your artwork with the bunny, fox and dinosaur hanging on my locker at the station."

"You *do*?" They could probably hear her delight all the way back to the pharmacy.

While Daisy was quizzing the other two men on whether the fire engines had multiple steering wheels, like the shopping cart race car, Will walked over to say hello to the other children, saving Megan for last. She had hoped that by the time he turned to her, she would have squashed her juvenile urge to blush. *So we kissed.* Was it really that big a deal?

Her gaze zeroed in on his mouth. *Yes*. Trying to sound like a responsible citizen and not a sex-starved deviant about to drag a firefighter behind the cantaloupes to have her way with him, she went with the time-honored and socially acceptable "Hi." If only she'd managed it without the squeak to her voice.

His self-assured grin told her that he'd heard it. "Just the woman I was hoping to see."

"Did you tail me to the grocery store? I'm pretty sure you're not allowed to use county rescue vehicles for stalking."

He laughed. "My being at the supermarket is strictly work-related. We make regular runs to stock up the station kitchen, but we're still on duty." He pointed to the radio he wore. "If a call comes in, we drop everything and go. Luckily, the store manager understands."

"So, why were you hoping to see me?"

"I have a couple of questions for you. First, and I meant to ask this last night, but got…distracted, what is a 'well-baby'? Apparently, Tommy has one on Monday."

"That's just a regularly scheduled pediatrician visit, not because the baby is sick, but because the doctor needs to monitor his growth and milestones. Like crawling." Tommy had actually made it a couple of inches yesterday before deciding it was too much work and collapsing on his tummy.

"Got it. Now that you explain it, it sounds so self-evident I feel stupid for asking. Question number two, want to be my date for Kate's wedding?"

"What?" She blinked, convinced she'd somehow misunderstood him. She'd been expecting another child-care inquiry. "But I—"

"Trent," one of the other firefighters boomed. "Are you coming or what?"

"There in a sec," Will called over his shoulder.

"We'll talk about this later, okay?" He turned toward his waiting crew members, one of whom was nudging the other with his elbow and smirking in Will's direction. "Oh, crap. One last thing, Megan. There's a distinct possibility that a few people around town have heard about our—"

"Mistletoe Moment?" she asked wryly. "Trust me, I'm aware."

His expression was sheepish. "Are you angry?"

"The last time I was the subject of any community gossip, it's because people felt sorry for the pregnant chick whose husband was screwing around on her—"

"That bastard!"

"—and they were speculating on how many lovers he had. So people chatting about the hottest guy in town kissing me is a step up."

His eyes crinkled at the corners. "You think I'm the hottest guy in town?"

"Mommy." There was a sharp tug at the hem of Megan's shirt, saving her from answering.

Grateful, Megan glanced down. "Yes, Daisy?"

"What's bast-ard?" Daisy asked, saying the word slowly as if testing it out.

"Oh no, honey, Mr. Will said… Um. Batard." She reached into the nearby bin of fresh-baked bread and pulled out of a loaf. "It's one of these. Here you go, Will."

Blue eyes laughing, he accepted it solemnly. "Thank you. Just what we need at the station. See you tonight, Daisy." To Megan, he said, "We can finish our discussion when I pick up Tommy."

Their discussion about whether or not she would be his date for the wedding?

There were multiple reasons why she should refuse. She was attending in a professional capacity. Mixing Will with business seemed potentially regrettable. Plus, weddings made her a little cranky; she wasn't far enough beyond her divorce not to wince at vows of fidelity and "death do us part." *So tell him no.* But if she said yes…the hottest guy in town might just kiss her again.

"LIKE THIS, BABY!" Iris got down on her hands and knees next to Tommy, demonstrating how to crawl. "I teaching him, Mommy."

"I see that," Megan said, supervising while she wrapped another strand of lights around the tree in the corner. They were saving the ornaments for after dinner.

Wanting to join in the fun, Lily dropped to all fours on Tommy's other side. But she quickly got distracted by pretending that she was a dog, barking and "digging." Rather than join in, Daisy looked mystified by the entire procedure.

"Why he not just walk?" she asked Megan.

"He'll get there eventually."

Daisy stuck her face down close to Tommy's. "You should walk."

He babbled happily at her.

"With feet," she clarified.

More babbling.

Shrugging, she retreated to her room with a selection of library books.

"Don't mind her," Megan told the baby. "Everyone's full of opinions. Best learn early not to take them too seriously." The phone in her jeans pocket rang. "See?

That's probably someone calling with an opinion now. Hello?"

"Hey." Just the sound of Will's voice made her grin. "How has your afternoon been? Kids driving you crazy?"

"Not really. Daisy attempted a short-lived career as a motivational speaker for infants, and Lily decided she's a dog. Pretty much the norm. What about you?"

"Well, I've left the station, but I'm not heading straight to the house yet. I have to pick up J— I have a stop to make. Is it okay if I'm fifteen or twenty minutes late?"

"Sure. If they haven't driven me to a mental breakdown by now, I'll probably be all right for another fifteen minutes." She sat on the couch, tucking her legs underneath her. "While I have you on the phone, I just wanted to say that I'm flattered you asked me to be your wedding date, but—"

"If you're going to be so cruel as to reject me, don't I deserve to hear it face-to-face? This is like dumping someone by text," he grumbled.

"It is not! For starters, I can't dump you. We were never dating." And she had opted to take advantage of this phone conversation because she wasn't sure she could turn him down face-to-face.

"Please, Megan. Go with me," he persisted.

"How about a compromise? We'll both be there anyway. I'll save you a dance."

He made a *phhbbt* sound, clearly not mollified. "You're an only child, right?"

"Yeah."

"I hope that you can understand this without thinking I'm a terrible brother, but Cole can be obnoxiously perfect. He's a great guy, always has been. He didn't beat up on his younger brothers, he didn't get in trouble, he made all A's. In comparison, I've always felt… I know this wedding day is about him and Kate, and I wish them all the happiness in the world, but there will be friends and family there looking at me, remembering my would-be wedding not too long ago."

He was embarrassed to go without a date.

As someone whose pride had taken more than a few hits over the last couple of years, she empathized. "But why me? There were half a dozen women at the Christmas tree farm you could have asked who won't be preoccupied with whether all the boutonnieres are pinned on straight or checking the arrangements every half hour to make sure nothing's wilting."

"I didn't want to give anyone the wrong impression. As Jace put it, a date to a wedding is a lot more romantic than, say, bowling. You know I'm not looking for a relationship. There *are* half a dozen women I could have asked, but I don't want to lead them on."

His blunt answer was a rather sobering reality check. What had she expected him to say? That he craved her company, that he wanted her to be his date because she was an excellent kisser? It was ludicrous that she could feel so let down when *she* had rejected *him*.

"Thank you for being candid with me. I just don't think I'm your girl. Confidentially—and please don't repeat this to any of my customer base—I don't like weddings. I mean, I do in theory. But I've only been to a few since I divorced my cheating husband, and I'm still a little raw. A little cynical. I caught myself rolling my eyes while a groom was saying his vows," she admitted.

"You think that's bad? I'm Cole's best man and I..."

The guilty edge to his voice made her rabidly curious. "Spill."

"I have these warped daydreams about him sneezing during his 'I do' or dropping the ring or something. Nothing that would mess up their big day, you understand, just a tiny flub. Something marginally less than perfect."

"Like the piano player hitting a wrong note."

"Exactly. Or a draft blowing out the unity candle."

"Or the minister getting their names wrong."

"Or the flower girl—"

"Hey, you leave all flower-related details out of this."

"Yes, ma'am. The flowers will be perfection."

"Hopefully, so will everything else. We're terrible people to even joke otherwise."

"Which is why we'd make excellent partners for this shindig. I'm going to win you over, you know."

"No, you aren't."

But he merely laughed as he ended the call.

After she put her phone back in her pocket, she kept replaying parts of their conversation, grinning. *He's a bad influence on you.* But she'd been the responsible, stable person who'd had to hold life together for her and the girls. The idea of being a little reckless was tantalizing. Maybe just for one night?

She was going to the wedding. There were worse ways to spend the evening than dancing with a sexy man who made her laugh. She'd have to find a dress and a sitter either way. Dagmar had said she'd watch the girls if the teenager down the street couldn't do it. *You know what Dagmar's vote would be.*

Then again, this was Megan's love life. Dagmar didn't get a vote.

The doorbell gargled its terrible death rattle, and she pressed her hand to her head. She really did need to look up online instructions for how to fix that. She did her usual workout routine of stepping over the waist-high baby gate—doing that a few hundred times a day had to be toning some muscles—and answered the door.

Her mouth dropped open in a gasp she tried to cover. "Mom!"

Beth Ann beamed at her. "Surprised, aren't you?"

"More than words can capture."

"Good news. I've come to stay with you for the week!"

Chapter Ten

Megan inhaled through her nose, and slowly exhaled, waiting for the fuzzy-headed faint feeling to subside. "Mom, what are you doing here?"

Beth Ann frowned. "I just told you, I've come to stay for the week. That way, I'll be out of your hair before Spencer arrives, but available to help you clean and get ready for Christmas." She hefted a plaid suitcase. "Now be a good girl and invite me in."

Megan could hardly tell her mother to get back in the car and hit the road. "Please. Do come in." She needed to get back to the living room anyway, to supervise the baby. No doubt her mother was going to have opinions about Megan watching Tommy.

It wasn't that she disliked her mom, exactly, but their personalities occasionally clashed. Beth Ann could fret over potential problems to the point that her worrying exhausted those around her, particularly her daughter who felt as if she should be doing more to allay her mother's concerns. Megan didn't have the energy or hours in the day to take care of herself, her daughters *and* her mother's worst-case scenarios.

"It's sweet that you came all this way, Mom," she

said, stepping over the baby gate. "But I'm not sure the timing—"

"How do you open this?" Beth Ann eyed the barrier as if it was a thing of evil. "The ones they had in my day weren't so complicated."

"Sorry." Megan reached down and released the spring-loaded latch. "As I was saying, as much as I appreciate your thoughtfulness—"

"Gammy!" Daisy came racing toward her grandmother for a hug.

Beth Ann looked momentarily terrified. She braced her hands out in front of her. "Slow down there, speedy. Gammy's no spring chicken. You don't want me to break a hip."

"Chicken?" Daisy threw her head back and laughed as if that were uproariously funny. Instead of tackling her grandmother, she grabbed her hand and tugged her into the living room. "Come see Iris and Lily and baby Tommy."

"Is Tommy your baby doll?"

Daisy laughed again. From her perspective, Gammy was a regular stand-up comedian. "No, baby Tommy is a baby."

Beth Ann's penciled eyebrows shot up, her quizzical gaze boring into Megan. "Did you get another one while I wasn't looking, dear?"

"Ha-ha. I'm babysitting for a neighbor." What were the chances that she could keep her mom from meeting said neighbor?

The last time they'd spoken on the phone, Beth Ann was espousing her long-held opinion that mothers should not be single. She firmly believed Megan needed a man in her life. If she found out that Megan's next-door neighbor was a virile firefighter who was good with children…

Fortunately, Tommy hadn't gotten into any trouble in the few minutes that Megan had taken her eyes off him. He was on his hands and knees, rocking back and forth and laughing at Iris.

Megan scooped him up. "I think it's about time for your bottle."

The girls had crowded around their grandmother, expressing affectionate greetings but also demanding to know if she had brought presents. Beth Ann unzipped her suitcase, pulling out a few brightly wrapped parcels.

"I do have gifts, but you can't open them until Christmas. Who wants to put them under the tree for Gammy?" She glanced at the spruce in the corner. "Oh. You haven't decorated yet."

"Nope, you're just in time," Megan said, shaking a bottle. "That's on our agenda for tonight."

"When you were younger," Beth Ann reminded her, "we always decorated the tree on December first. It was a family tradition."

"I'm all for tradition, but I've been a little busy, Mom."

"I can imagine." Her mother sat next to her on the couch. "What with that flower stuff you do—"

"My job."

"—and the girls. And now you're taking in other children on top of that?"

Only my mom could make a single baby sound like I'm running a home for juvenile delinquents. "The extra cash is nice at the holidays."

Her mother pursed her lips. "Are you having money troubles, dear? That rat Spencer—"

"Ixnay on the at-ray." Megan cast a meaningful glance at her daughters. She tried never to speak ill of their father in front of them.

"I'm sorry." Beth Ann lowered her voice to just above a whisper. "But it makes me so mad, him cavorting with Barbie or Bunny—"

"I think he said Bonnie."

"—while you're here spending Christmas *alone*." She practically wailed the word.

"Well, Spencer and I aren't married anymore. He's legally allowed to cavort. And I'm not lonely. I have the girls and Dagmar." And the dangerously attractive next-door neighbor who was either a blessing or a bad influence. The jury was still out.

Beth Ann patted her knee. "And also me. That's why I'm here, to help you get ready for Christmas."

Megan adjusted Tommy in her arms, giving her mother a knowing look over the baby's head. "Are you sure you aren't here to criticize my life choices?"

"I can multitask, dear."

Megan wasn't sure whether to laugh or to be very afraid. The doorbell wheezed, and her heart jumped to her throat. Will! How quickly could she hand off the baby and send them on their way without being unforgivably rude?

"Do you want me to answer that?" her mother offered.

But Megan was already bolting from the sofa, holding Tommy tight against her while she cleared the gate. "Coming!"

As she reached for the doorknob, her mind scrambled for a plan of action. Personally, she thought Will had a fantastic family, but Gayle Trent could, on occasion, get a little intense about wanting what was best for her sons. So perhaps Megan could make him understand, quickly and quietly, why he should avoid her matrimonial-minded mother.

She opened the door as narrowly as possible. "Hey, just a heads-up—"

Will beamed at her, like a little boy with a secret he couldn't wait share. "Do you have a few minutes?"

"Actually, this isn't the best time…" How best to encapsulate Beth Ann without using words that would upset her mother too much if she overheard?

"Oh." His face fell. "Want me to tell Santa to hit the bricks, then?"

"Santa." She opened the door farther and craned her head outside the door to spot a Santa Claus standing on her sidewalk.

His demeanor seemed more sarcastic than jolly, but he gamely offered a "Ho-ho-ho."

"My brother Jace," Will explained softly.

"Nice to meet you," Jace said. "I know it's hard to tell right now, but I'm the good-looking Trent. I'm also, unfortunately, the Trent who is *not* too tall to fit the suit." He shot his brother a glare beneath his fake bushy eyebrows, an adorably malevolent Father Christmas. It was clear Will had coerced him into being here.

For my girls. Her heart melted. The triplets still hadn't seen Santa this year. Leave it to Will, who was fast becoming one of her daughters' favorite people, to arrange a house call.

Hell, she was going to have to introduce him to her

mom. There was no way she could send him away in light of his thoughtfulness.

"Megan?" her mother prodded from the hallway. "Who's at the door?"

Someone very special. Her gaze locked with Will's, and she blurted under her breath, "Yes, I'll be your date for the wedding."

"Oh, *he* gets a date out of this?" Jace drawled.

"You get my everlasting gratitude." She blew him a kiss. "And a lifetime discount on flowers, should you ever want to impress a special lady friend."

Will stepped forward and squeezed her hand. "I would have worn you down—I'm very persuasive—but I wouldn't have used the girls to do it. This is for them, not to impress you."

"I know." Which was why she was moved by the gesture.

"Where are the girls?" he asked in a low voice. "Usually, they're crowding around to say hi. Did you say it was a bad time because someone's asleep? Sick?"

"No, they're just momentarily distracted by my mother. Who arrived unexpectedly." She tried to apologize with her eyes for whatever Beth Ann might say. "Do you two want to come in, or should I bring the girls out here?"

Will glanced at his brother. "Do you mind staying put for a minute?"

"For the record, you owe me so big. When I get married, you are paying for the bachelor party. And it will be epic."

Will and Megan went into the house, and she

passed him Tommy. "His crawling is getting really good."

"Tell me about it. I may need to buy baby gates this weekend." He stopped, looking dazed. "I can't believe that sentence just came out of my mouth." Shaking it off, he walked into the living room. "You must be Megan's mom. I'm Will Trent, her neighbor."

"*You* live next door to my daughter?" Beth Ann eyed him with the same gleeful avarice Daisy had shown for the toy catalog that came in the mail last week. "I think it's wonderful that you two single parents could help each other out."

Megan almost snorted at her mother's abrupt change of heart.

"I'm actually not a parent—long story—but I couldn't agree more about your daughter being wonderful. Will you excuse me a moment?" He turned toward her daughters. "Iris? Do you remember we talked about you drawing a picture for Santa, and I promised you'd get a chance to meet him?"

She nodded eagerly.

"Did you draw your picture? Can you go get it?"

From the speed with which she dashed to her room and back, no one would ever guess that she was the slowest one to leave the house each morning. When she tried to hand the drawing over to him, he grinned. "No, you hold on to that. I have a surprise for you— all three of you. I sent Santa an email telling him how sad you were that you didn't get to meet him, and he asked if he could come visit you sometime. Would that be okay?"

Daisy and Iris both shouted, "Yes!" loudly enough to make their grandmother wince.

"Would you like to meet him now?" Will asked. Another volley of yeses followed. He paused for a moment, studying each girl, then went back to the front door.

"How about we wait over by the Christmas tree?" Megan suggested so that Iris and Daisy didn't both ambush Santa at once. Will's brother might not know what he was in for. Will returned with Jace and a chair from the kitchen.

Whether Jace was here voluntarily or not, he certainly put his heart into it. "Ho-ho-ho! Merry Christmas, Rivers family," he boomed.

Lily and Iris gasped. Daisy shouted back, "Merry Christmas!"

Will set the chair by the fireplace while Daisy asked Santa if he'd brought his reindeer.

Jace shook his head. "No, they're all being checked out by the North Pole veterinarian. He's the doctor who makes sure they're healthy enough to fly all over the world."

"I hafta go to the doctor sometimes," Daisy commiserated. "I don't like shots."

"Neither do the reindeer. Rudolph got so mad that his nose turned a whole bunch of different colors! It glowed yellow for a week."

The girls giggled.

Jace sat in the chair. "I thought I'd visit today so you girls could tell me some of the things you might like for Christmas. Then maybe your mommy can take some pictures?" He turned toward Iris. "Speaking of pictures, the elves told me that you made something for me."

Her eyes grew wide. "They did?" She raced forward to show him the drawing, the piece of paper flapping like it was caught in a wind tunnel.

He made such a fuss over her artistic skills that Lily and Daisy both ran for the crayon box. Megan bit the inside of her cheek to keep from laughing. If Jace wasn't careful, he'd leave here today with enough drawings to wallpaper his house. He addressed each girl by name without ever asking who was who, and she realized that Will must've described what they were wearing, thinking ahead to add a bit more magic to the visit. Her eyes burned. *Get a grip—you're not really about to cry over a bartender in a Santa suit, are you?*

No, if she shed any tears, it would be over the kindness Will had shown them. One of Megan's greatest concerns in life was how uninvolved Spencer was with his daughters; obviously, distance and job concerns were factors, but the truth was, he didn't expend much effort. She'd worried that as the girls grew older they might notice that more, might take it personally. Might feel unloved. But family could mean lots of things, not all definitions biological. She suddenly felt more confident that here in Cupid's Bow, there would be enough special people to make up for Spencer's lack.

Will caught her eye, and his grin faltered. He mouthed the words *you okay?* She nodded, redoubling her efforts to keep her composure. For months after moving here, she'd foolishly scoffed at women who threw themselves at Will because of his deep blue eyes and muscular body. But she now realized there were so many reasons a woman would want him.

Recalling their kiss, she admitted to herself that *she* wanted him.

Enough to do anything about it? Probably not. Even if she would be content with a casual affair, it wasn't as if she could seduce him in the kitchen while the girls sang along to a nursery rhyme CD in the next room. *But if you had a real opportunity?*

That was such a dangerous thought she decided to busy herself with something else. "Time for pictures, okay? Then we should let Santa go. He has a lot to do in order to get ready for Christmas." Daisy and Iris both climbed into his lap and were already saying "Cheese!" before Megan even had her phone out. Lily stood next to Santa's chair, not touching him but looking otherwise happy and relaxed.

Megan got a number of great shots, and Jace rewarded the girls by distributing candy canes and stickers. By the time he stood to go, he'd committed so fully to his role that Megan couldn't find any traces of the grumbling smart aleck she'd met earlier. Cupid's Bow Community Theater could benefit from his talents.

Jace left first, presumably disappearing into his brother's house, and Will left a few minutes later so that it wasn't immediately obvious that he needed to give Santa a ride home.

She walked Will to the door. "They're going to be talking about this for days. They'll be the envy of the entire preschool. Thank you." She looked up at his handsome face and knew that, if he hadn't been holding a baby right then, she would have kissed him. "You're a hell of a guy, Will Trent."

He gave her a lazy grin. "I have my moments."

Closing the door behind him, she turned to find her mother, a gleam in her eye.

"Well, well, well. That was certainly a surprise."

"Yeah. Who could have anticipated a drop-in from Saint Nick?"

"The bigger surprise was that strapping young gentleman you've never bothered to mention during any of our phone conversations."

She sighed. "Will is a complicated subject, and… I need to get dinner started."

On the bright side, if her mother was still here next Saturday, she gave every indication that she would be happy to babysit the girls during the wedding. From the way Beth Ann had ogled Will—as if he was the answer to her prayers—she'd be more than happy to babysit if he wanted to take Megan on an expedition to the actual North Pole. Later, Megan would have to find a tactful way to explain to her mom that there was no future with Will.

In the meantime, Megan needed to remind herself of that. As often as possible.

WILL QUICKLY SURVEYED the premises, as he'd been trained to do, and realized he should have called for backup. His nerves were taut with trepidation. He fought the urge to bolt for the exit. Trying to put on a brave face, he told Tommy, "We'll get through this together."

Glancing up from his car seat, the baby responded with "B-b-b-b." Which was probably infant-speak for *Dude, how about we just bail and go for a walk in the park? No one has to know.*

The bright, primary colors of the pediatric wait-

ing room were almost ominously cheerful—like a
nightmare about clowns. The room was packed with
beleaguered-looking mothers of children who ran the
gamut from hyperactive to plague-stricken. A kid in
the corner was coughing all over everyone in a three-
foot radius, reminding Will uneasily of a medical
thriller he'd seen about a futuristic pandemic.

"Don't worry," he muttered to Tommy. "We're not
sitting anywhere near Patient Zero over there." Will
didn't really want to sit in this room, period. Once
he'd checked in with the receptionist, couldn't she
give him the kind of buzzer popular restaurants used
on crowded nights? Then he and Tommy could wait
in his comparatively germ-free car until the buzzer lit
up, alerting them that their table—er, exam room—
was ready.

He filled out some forms at the front window, and
the receptionist told him to "take a seat." Sadly, she
neither handed him a buzzer nor told him he could
wait at the bar. So Will folded himself into a va-
cant chair that seemed more appropriately sized for
a six-year-old than a six-foot-plus man. The assorted
magazines fanned across the table had bold-faced
headlines on bed-wetting, breast-feeding and baby
names. He grimaced.

My kingdom for a Sports Illustrated.

He didn't mind bringing Tommy to the doctor;
he would do anything he could to keep the little guy
healthy. But he regretted not asking someone to ac-
company him—Megan, or Kate, or Megan, or his
mom. Or Megan. Like a kid replaying his favorite
part of the movie over and over, he thought once again
of the look she'd given him last Friday when he'd

brought Jace over. She'd beamed at Will as if he were a superhero, one she wanted to cover with kisses. Would she give him any of those kisses at the wedding on Saturday? He—

His pleasant daydreams were harshly interrupted when an elementary-aged kid ran over to the nearby garbage can and vomited.

"I am so sorry," the kid's mother said. "There was someone in the bathroom, and, as you can see, it was an emergency. Can we get a bottle of water?" she called to a nurse behind the counter.

Will moved to another section of the wall in order to give his chair to the still-green-faced kid. A mother two seats down was wagging her finger at her daughter, threatening, "Wait until your father hears about this. I'm tempted to call him right now at work. He's going to want to have a *long* talk with you when he gets home tonight."

Will felt a twinge of sympathy for the unseen father. Somewhere, the man was probably working hard at his job, waiting for Monday to end, with no idea that he'd just been scheduled to preside over a disciplinary hearing. It struck Will that if you were a parent, you never really went home from work. Your work was ongoing from the moment a child was born to…well, forever, based on his own mother. She certainly hadn't stopped fretting over her sons just because they no longer lived at home. The responsibilities were unending, from grocery trips to laundry loads to soccer practices to ballet recitals to doctor appointments to homework assistance to bedtime stories to last-minute checks under beds and in closets for monsters.

He rocked the car seat in his lap, reaching out his hand so that Tommy could grab his fingers. "No offense, little man, but I'll be glad when your mama gets back. You're fun to hang out with—come visit when you're older and I'll teach you to ride a horse and fish—but I'd like my life back." Over the weekend, after he'd finished with the charity light display, Manuel and Brody had gone for beers and to shoot pool. They'd invited Will to go along, but he'd felt obligated to get Tommy home to bed.

"Tommy Reynolds?" A nurse in her late forties, dressed in Christmas-themed scrubs, read the name off a clipboard from a side doorway.

"That's us. Him, I mean." Will stood and crossed the waiting room.

"Right this way."

They went down a long hallway, and she stopped at the end to get Tommy's height and weight. Then she settled them into an exam room.

"Is there a little paper gown I'm supposed to dress him in?" Will joked.

She laughed, then told him he wouldn't have to wait long for Dr. Ingram. Half an hour later, Will was thinking that the kind-faced nurse might actually be a pathological liar. Thirty minutes was like nine hours in baby time. Tommy was starting to get antsy, no longer entertained by his ring of plastic keys, his favorite puppy blanket or Will's repertoire of funny faces. Will had pulled the baby out of the car seat and was bouncing him on his lap. What Tommy really wanted was to be let down to scoot across the tile floor, which Will thought was a bad idea. *Hurry up*, he silently implored the doctor.

As if responding to the mental plea, a slender woman with close-cropped hair and wide hazel eyes suddenly entered the room. She quirked an eyebrow at him. "You're not Amy."

"Not last time I checked. She's out of town, and I'm watching Tommy." He held out his hand. "Will Trent."

"Darcy Ingram. Nice to meet you." She paused, studying him. "Have you and Amy been dating long?"

"Oh, we're just friends. I'm not dating anyone." The words were reflexive, not meant to hint that he was available, but her expression shifted, reflecting interest.

His answering smile was ambivalent. She was attractive, an intelligent and clearly successful woman, but he had no interest in flirting with her. He just wanted to get through this appointment and—

Who am I? Since when did he purchase baby gates and stop showing interest in women?

"Mr. Trent, are you all right?"

Not really. He felt disoriented and uncomfortably flushed. *Probably caught the flu in that waiting room.* "Right as rain."

She examined Tommy, asking about his feeding schedule, sleep habits and motor skills. Will reported the crawling with a boastful smile, as if it was something he personally had accomplished. She proclaimed the baby healthy but noted that he had a touch of eczema, and then she told Will it was time to start introducing solid foods.

"You should begin with an iron-fortified, single-grain cereal. Once his teeth come in, which should be soon, and he develops some chewing skills, we can start slowly adding mashed fruit and veggies. We have a nurses' hotline if you have any questions or if he has any bad reactions." Her brisk, professional tone grew huskier. "Or I can give you my cell phone number."

"I doubt that will be necessary. I live next door to an unofficial baby expert." He would call Megan to ask about what cereal and feeding supplies to buy for Tommy. When he realized just how much he was looking forward to talking to her, he almost groaned.

It had been weeks since he felt any interest in another woman, yet he kept dwelling on one he'd barely kissed—one whose life was full of those parenting responsibilities he'd been lamenting earlier. *Times three.*

Megan Rivers was not the kind of woman he normally dated, yet he was as excited about her accompanying him to Cole's wedding as he was about the fact that his brother was getting married. Which might actually be more disconcerting than the pediatric waiting room.

WHEN THE DRYER buzzer sounded Wednesday evening, Megan sprang up from her seat at the table. She realized that she'd been unconsciously listening for the signal, impatiently waiting for it.

"That means Tommy's puppy blanket is dry," she said to no one in particular. The combination stuffed animal/security blanket had had a rough day, first taking the brunt of Iris's juice, then being part of a diaper-related accident. It had been in the wash when Will picked up the baby earlier. "I'd better run it next door. Tommy loves his blanket. I'm sure Will needs it before bedtime."

She hurried from the room before her mother could comment. Will had become a touchy subject. Over the weekend, Megan had explained to her mother that Will was counting the days until Amy returned for her son and he could return to an uncomplicated bachelor existence, thus ruling him out as marriage material for a mother of three. She hadn't been sure her protests would actually dissuade her mom. But then yesterday, her mother had gone into town to have lunch with Dagmar and had apparently run into Will with the baby.

"It was disgusting," Beth Ann had sniffed later. "He was *surrounded* by women. He was obviously exploiting the baby to pick up dates. You were right to avoid dating him, dear. He's just like Spencer, probably never satisfied with just one woman's attention."

Megan had mixed feelings about her mother's new dislike of him. Her gut reaction had been to defend him. After all, she'd seen firsthand at the Christmas tree farm that women surrounding him wasn't always the result of something he'd done. If he wanted female attention, he didn't have to use a cute baby to get it—although she could personally attest to the *aww* factor of watching him and Tommy together. But rather than speak up on his behalf, Megan had held her tongue. It suited her purposes for her mother to back off from the idea of a neighborhood romance.

Beth Ann had been rather frosty when she opened the door for him earlier; he'd left the minute he had Tommy's stuff in hand. With her mom here, Megan hadn't been talking to him as much. There had been no staying for dinner or exchanging bad jokes about harmless wedding mishaps. Toasty warm baby blanket in hand, she welcomed the opportunity to go catch up. *Catch up on what, exactly? You see the man practically every day. Nothing earth-shattering has happened that you need to report.*

But she missed him. That was the bald truth. She crossed their yards with purpose. As she rapped against his front door, she realized that the last time she'd been here was to complain about the car alarm. She seemed to recall that she'd made some acerbic remarks about his dates. And as of this Saturday, she would be one of his dates. She couldn't wait to see his reaction to the dress she'd splurged on at Jasmine Tucker's boutique.

"Yeah?" The door swung open, and Will stood there wearing an irritated expression and multiple splotches of baby cereal across the front of his T-shirt.

Been there. "Did I interrupt in the middle of dinnertime?"

"Hard to say. Dinner implies food. I've been too preoccupied with Tommy to fix anything for myself, and I'm not sure I've successfully got any food into him. Mostly, it seems to be all over his face and me. Come on in. Just don't tell my mother that the place is a mess and that I didn't have any refreshments to offer you. Gayle Trent takes hospitality very seriously."

"I won't rat you out to your mom," she promised. "After all, I'm partly here to hide from mine. And to give you this." She started to hand him the freshly laundered puppy blanket but, seeing the cereal smears across his knuckles and wrist, opted to set it on the back of the sofa instead. "Want some help?"

"God, yes." He ran his non-cereal-encrusted hand through his dark hair. "But what I really want is for Amy to come back. I'm not cut out for this long-term."

"If it makes you feel any better, I think all parents feel that way at some point. Even those of us who really, *really* wanted kids."

"I know you're probably telling the truth, but the way I feel right at this moment, it's tough to imagine I'll ever want kids."

"How about you let me feed Tommy, and you can put some dinner together for yourself? I bet your outlook will improve once you have some food in your system."

"Wise words."

She went into the kitchen, where Tommy was strapped into a high chair. "Kate went with me to the store to pick it out," he said. "I had actually been thinking about asking you to come with me for guidance, but…"

"But?"

He shook his head. "Nothing. I don't know. Hunger's making me light-headed. I guess you're already doing so much for us, and I didn't want to…become too dependent."

"It's been a two-way street," she reminded him. He had tackled a couple of minor outdoor chores for her and even mentioned he might be able to fix the doorbell. "But I know what you mean." Since the divorce, it hadn't been easy to ask for help. She'd felt as if she'd needed to prove her self-reliance.

While Will puttered around in the kitchen behind her, she took over the task of feeding Tommy. She assumed that Will's future sister-in-law had also helped him pick out baby-friendly dishes and the soft-tipped spoon Tommy was currently gumming.

"This will get easier," she told Will. "He's still learning how to eat off a utensil, which is different than the sucking reflex he's used to."

"So mealtimes will stop being so damnably messy and counterproductive?"

"Don't be ridiculous. You've been to my house for dinner—I think feeding the kids stays messy and aggravating until roughly college."

He laughed at that, finally sounding more like himself. He ate his dinner standing at the counter, and once they began laughing and chatting, the time flew. As she was rinsing out Tommy's bowl, her gaze landed on the oven clock.

She blinked. "I've been here an hour?"

"Has it been that long?" His expression mirrored her own surprise. "Sorry—didn't mean to keep you."

She smiled at him. "I'm not sorry." Would he think it was stupid if she said she'd had fun? Spoon-feeding a six-month-old rice cereal was not exactly a hot date, but Will's company left her with warm tingles and a grin that stayed on her face as she walked back to her house, humming softly.

Her mother met her in the foyer. "The girls are putting on their pajamas. I wasn't sure when you were coming back. I had no idea it took so long to return a baby blanket."

"He needed help feeding Tommy."

"Don't let that man use you, Megan. He's just like Spencer, a charmer. I'm sure he knows how to manipulate that charm to—"

"He is *nothing* like Spencer. There is more thoughtfulness and kindness in Will Trent's little finger than my ex-husband had."

"Oh no," Beth Ann breathed, pressing a hand to her midsection. "This is worse than I thought. You have feelings for him."

"Yes. Friendly, neighborly feelings." She went into the kitchen to fill the teakettle, hoping in vain that going into a different room would end the conversation.

Her mother followed after her. "You're going to get in over your head. Spencer's affairs injured your pride, and I understand that a fling is probably a wonderful pick-me-up—"

"Will is not a fling. No one's getting flung, Mother."

"—but you have three impressionable daughters to think about. They have to come before hormones and a hot fireman."

Megan slammed the kettle onto the stove and whirled around. "Are you suggesting that I don't put those girls first? That I don't think every day about how they're dependent on me? Because—"

"You're a good mother," Beth Ann said softly. "I didn't mean to suggest otherwise. But a man like Will Trent could turn a woman's head. Make sure yours is clear." With that, she went to check on the girls to make sure bedtime preparations hadn't turned into a toothpaste free-for-all.

Megan's earlier good mood had evaporated like

steam from the kettle. Her mother was overbearing and prone to negativity. But she wasn't entirely wrong. Will Trent could definitely turn a woman's head.

Except it wasn't her head Megan was worried about.

Chapter Eleven

As she scurried around her room in her bathrobe, Megan felt like an actress who was about to play two roles in the same production. Today was the wedding. Megan needed to get to the church early for setup, and she was also packing a bag and cosmetics so that she could change later. Kate had invited her to use the bridal rooms where she, Crystal and Sierra would be getting ready.

Megan shimmied into a pair of jeans and an elegant gold sweater, making a mental checklist of everything she still needed to do. *For starters, blow-dry your hair.* The wet strands clinging to her face made it hard to see what accessories she was grabbing.

But no sooner had she turned on the hair dryer than there was a knock at her bedroom door.

Great. No doubt her mother wanted to get in one last lecture. Although she hadn't said anything derogatory about Will in front of the girls, who adored him, she'd mumbled a few snide comments to Megan—including an innuendo-laden report of a pretty woman showing up on his doorstep. Half wondering if Amy had returned, Megan had glanced out the window, then laughed. "That's Kate, the woman marrying his brother. Quit trying to create scandals."

"Megan?" her mom called through the closed door.

She briefly considered pretending that she hadn't heard Beth Ann over the dryer. *Don't be passive-aggressive. You're better than that.* Probably.

"I'm a little busy," she hollered back, "so if—"

Her mom opened the door and poked her head inside, her expression troubled. "You have a phone call," she said apologetically. "Spencer."

The last thing Megan wanted to do right now was speak to her faithless ex-husband, but this might be important. He was scheduled to arrive the day after tomorrow. She reached for the extension on her nightstand. "Thanks, Mom. I've got it." She waited until her mother had closed the door and moved away. "Spencer? This is unexpected."

"Hi, Meggie. We need to talk about my visit next week."

Her grip tightened on the phone, her stomach churning. "Your daughters never get to see you. So help me, if you are canceling on them—"

"Just the opposite," he interrupted. "I thought about it, and I agree it's important I spend Christmas Day with them. Like you originally invited me to do. Bonnie convinced me it would be the right thing."

Stop grinding your teeth. Just because her ex was a wishy-washy adulterer who prioritized his girlfriend's opinion over his parenting responsibilities was no reason to cause herself dental damage. "As I recall, Bonnie was why you couldn't come on Christmas Day. Big of her to change her mind."

"There's no need for the waspish tone. You're getting exactly what you wanted."

No, dumb-ass. What I wanted was a husband who stuck to his vows. In a perfect world, they would have spent this and future Christmases as an intact family.

"I do have one condition," he continued. "I want Bonnie to come with me."

She made a gurgling sound, choking on her laughter. Or outrage. "You want to bring your girlfriend to spend Christmas at my house."

"Bonnie and I are very serious about each other. We'll spend Christmas morning with her parents, then drive to Cupid's Bow. If all goes well, by that afternoon, she won't just be my girlfriend. She'll be my fiancée."

Megan's stomach plummeted. She dimly realized her hands were shaking. It wasn't that she still had tender feelings for Spencer; her reaction stemmed from shock. For the last couple of years of their marriage, he'd shown so little respect for the institution that it had never occurred to her he might one day try it again.

"Megan?" he asked softly. "I know this probably comes as a surprise—"

"You *think*?"

"I screwed up our marriage, and as a result I lost you and the girls. I want to be a better man, I want to get it right the next time. Bonnie is my fresh start."

She kept to herself the rather cynical observation that it sounded as if he wanted Bonnie more for what she represented than out of deep and abiding love. "For the record, Spencer, you didn't *lose* your girls. They are here, and they deserve to have a fa-

ther. I never tried to stop you from contacting them
or spending time with them. In fact, I've encouraged
it." Adamantly.

"I know. You've been great about everything.
Which is why I felt comfortable asking if I could
bring Bonnie. I mean, it only makes sense for them
to meet their future stepmother."

I can't believe he's doing this at Christmas. Was
Megan just supposed to invite the woman who was replacing her into her home and have a holly, jolly time?

Then again, how could she be astounded by Spencer's
selfishness? It was completely true to character. "Bring
her, but the two of you will have to find a hotel for the
night. You won't be staying here."

"Of course not, wouldn't dream of it. I'm so glad
we worked this out! It's a blessing to know you're not
going to be difficult about my moving forward with
my life. And don't worry, Megan." His voice oozed
what was probably meant to be friendly support. "I'm
sure you'll be moving on with your own life before
you know it."

He was so lucky that she had over a week to calm
down. If he'd been in the room with her right at that
moment, she would've congratulated him on his engagement with her knee.

As SHE'D TOLD WILL, Megan had temporarily lost some
of her joy in weddings. And as she stomped up the
sidewalk toward the church, still irate over her phone
call from Spencer, she was afraid that today might
be worse than usual. But as soon as she began un-
packing flowers and netting and greenery, her mood
lifted. Not just because she loved her job, although

she did, but because she recalled Kate's enthusiasm as she had picked out each arrangement and bud. Kate was a wonderful woman, who deserved a lifetime of happiness, and despite Megan's occasional cynical moments, she believed down to her bones that Cole would provide that.

The men of the world could learn something from the Trent brothers, Megan decided, thinking of Jace's kindness to her girls when he'd been their Santa Claus and all of the times Will had brightened her day. She made a vow to herself right then and there: *today* would be bright. Not just for the bride and groom, but for Megan. While she hadn't appreciated Spencer's condescending remark about her moving forward, she refused to dwell on her past. She might never be ready for a step like Kate and Cole were taking, joining their families and planning a forever future, but she wanted to be more than a divorced woman whose self-esteem had been rocked by her husband's cheating.

She would be spending the day with people she really liked, her date was drop-dead sexy—imagining him in his tux made her toes curl—and she had free babysitting. What more could a single mom ask for? Her mother had cautioned that Will was not the kind of man with whom she could have a future. Maybe not. But perhaps there was something to be said for slowing down and taking a little more time to enjoy the present.

THE WEDDING WAS PERFECT. Megan sat in the pew with a lump in her throat from the moment Alyssa and Mandy walked down the aisle, identical flower girls beaming with happiness that their father was about to marry Kate. Although Kate's teenage son was far past the traditional age of a ring bearer, Luke had also been included in the ceremony. He and Deputy Thomas were both acting as ushers and had seated special guests prior to the ceremony

Next came Sierra Bailey, bridesmaid, and Crystal Walsh, matron of honor, but even though Megan should be watching them, her gaze kept straying to the front of the sanctuary where Will stood with his brothers. All three were handsome men, but in her opinion, Will's appeal was unmatchable.

He looked every bit as delectable in his tuxedo as she had predicted, and judging by his dazed reaction when they'd run into each other outside the sanctuary earlier, he liked how she looked, too. The tailoring of her green dress was very flattering and, after so many days of jeans and sneakers, the low back that left her shoulder blades exposed felt glamorously daring. Before the ceremony, Sierra had helped her curl her thick, dark hair and pin it to one side. Sierra had also let her borrow jeweled chandelier earrings that were far more dazzling than the pair Megan had planned to wear.

The service was brief, eloquent in its simplicity. This was the second marriage for both Kate and Cole, and they knew what was at stake, understood what being married meant. They exchanged vows that they had written, and nobody sneezed or stumbled. Megan was glad. Moments of perfection were rare in life, and they'd earned this one. As Will looked on, so visibly happy for his brother, she knew that in spite of any previous joking around, he wanted this to be flawless for them, too.

After Cole kissed the bride, he spun toward the guests with a mischievous smile. "I don't know about the rest of you, but I'm ready to celebrate!"

Applause filled the room, and the organist began playing the recessional.

The reception was being held at the Cupid's Bow Country Club; Megan had coordinated centerpieces and other decorations with the staff there. In the crush of people exiting the sanctuary, Will grabbed her hand.

"Do you want to ride over with me?" he asked, lacing his fingers through hers as if it was the most natural thing in the world.

"Absolutely." She wanted to say something clever or flirty, but she was so full of emotion that casual conversation wouldn't quite come.

The short drive across town was quiet, but not awkward. She and Will kept exchanging smiles, stealing glances. She'd gaze sidelong in his direction and catch him doing the same. She knew she was grinning like an idiot. "You're staring."

"Busted. Just so you know, it's extremely difficult to keep my eyes on the road when I'm sitting next to such a beautiful woman."

She smoothed her hands over her skirt, loving the satiny feel against her skin. "It's the dress." Jasmine was a genius with fashion, and the boutique splurge had been worth it.

Will pulled his car into the country-club parking lot. "It's the woman. Trust me." He took the key out of the ignition but didn't reach for his car door. Instead, he reached for her. He stroked one hand over her shoulder, and ripples of pleasure went through her body. "I know we have to go inside, but once we do, we're subject to everybody else's opinions and scrutiny. When I kissed you at the Christmas tree farm, I wasn't thinking about witnesses or local gossip. I was only thinking about your mouth."

Liquid heat melted through her. In response to his words, her gaze locked on his lips. To heck with the reception. There was no place she'd rather be than in this car, in Will's arms.

"I don't want to do anything in there that will make you the object of public speculation, but, Megan, I've needed to kiss you since the minute I saw you today."

She cupped his face in her hands, sliding a finger over his strong cheekbone, admiring his hard jaw, and leaned into him. This was not a sweet Mistletoe Moment fit for onlookers. This was repressed desire finally free to express itself.

How many times had she thought about kissing Will again? The reality of it was hotter and deeper than her imaginings. When his tongue teased over her lips and swept into her mouth, she moaned her encouragement for more. Heat pooled between her thighs, in her breasts, the tips hardened, aching for his touch. The sheer wantonness of her response shocked her. On some level, she recognized that even though it was dark outside, she and Will were still visible beneath the parking lot lights. But that didn't seem like enough motivation to quit kissing him.

He was the one who finally found the self-control to end the kiss. She clutched the front of his jacket in protest, but he was already tracing his lips over the sensitive curve of her neck, and she trembled in renewed pleasure.

When he reached between them to palm her breast, she almost cried out. *Too much.* She started to swat his hand away but then raised it to her mouth and kissed his fingertips instead. Were the windows starting to fog?

"We've got to stop, or we'll miss the reception."

He nipped at her earlobe. "I'll pay for their honeymoon."

Her laugh was ragged. "We have to go inside. You have to give a toast."

"Fine, but it's your fault if the toast is incoherent. I don't have enough blood left in my brain to string sentences together."

"It will be better once we get out of the car," she said, trying to convince herself as much as him. "Then you'll be able to think clearly."

He gave her a final, searing kiss. "Just for the record, I haven't been able to think clearly since I realized you were standing under mistletoe. I doubt I'll start now."

IT WAS LATE, but nobody seemed to want to leave. Megan could empathize. When was the last time she'd had so much fun? Champagne had been flowing freely, Jace had been cracking her up with childhood stories about Will and she'd danced for two hours. Her shoes were under a chair somewhere, and she'd borrowed an elastic band from Anita Drake to loop her hair into a ponytail once she started to perspire. Megan was hot and sticky and deliriously happy.

Even though Kate and Cole weren't leaving for their honeymoon until the day after Christmas, Megan was sure the newlyweds must be eager to be alone. So she wasn't surprised when the DJ made the announcement that it was time for the bride to throw her bouquet. "Will all of the unmarried women take the floor?"

Ladies ranging from their twenties to their sixties— including Dagmar—headed for the center of the room. Standing to the side, Megan grinned.

Kate tugged at her arm. "What are you waiting for, unmarried woman?"

Megan blinked in surprise. "I'm not part of this, I *made* the bouquet."

"Come on, it's my wedding day. Don't be a spoil-sport."

Megan humored her by joining the throng, but stayed toward the back edge. She had no intention of embarrassing herself by diving for those flowers. Even though the whole tradition was a silly supersti-tion, she hoped Sierra caught the arrangement. She was clearly smitten with Jarrett Ross, and more en-gagements meant more weddings, which was good for business.

Town librarian Hadley Lanier was also hovering at the outskirts. The pretty young woman winked at Megan. "It's safer back here. You do not want to get between Becca Johnston and those flowers."

"Is she that eager to remarry?" Megan knew that, like her, the town councilwoman had gotten a divorce sometime during the last few years.

"She's just very goal-oriented. I don't think it mat-ters whether the goal is getting the council to vote in her favor or catching flowers."

"Ah."

The DJ played a prerecorded drumroll, and Kate launched the bouquet.

From the crowd, Jace whistled. "With an arm like that, why isn't she on the church softball team?"

Megan had turned automatically toward the sound of his voice and didn't realize the flowers were sailing at her head until it was practically too late. She held up her hands to protect her face, and the crowd cheered.

"Congratulations," Hadley said.

"Thanks." *But I don't want these.* They were a symbol of the future, and she wasn't ready to think about that right now. Was it so wrong to savor the moment?

Then again, the moment was ending. She knew it was almost time to leave. After the crowd of well-wishers had seen Kate and Cole to their car, she returned inside to find her shoes. It was like Cinderella in reverse. Slipping her foot into her glass slippers—okay, fine, beaded three-inch pumps—signaled the arrival of an unwanted midnight.

As they walked to the car, Will settled his tuxedo jacket over her shoulders and she cast him a grateful smile. "I had a wonderful time tonight," she said softly. "I'm glad that you asked me, and that you didn't give up when I tried to turn you down."

He grinned. "I'm glad I didn't give up, too."

They listened to the radio on the way home, and Megan closed her eyes, enjoying these last tranquil minutes.

"Sleepy?" he asked her.

"No, just content. Or…almost content. I'm not

ready for the night to end yet. I wish I could invite you in."

"I understand. Your mom might be waiting up for you. I'm sure she'll want to hear about the wedding."

"Or issue more dire warnings about you." Damn. She hadn't meant to say that. The late hour and four glasses of champagne she'd enjoyed made it more difficult to censor her words.

"She barely even knows me."

"Yes, well. She's formed some conclusions." Like mother, like daughter, Megan thought wryly. "She seems to think you have some lusty ulterior motives."

"Guilty." He pulled into the driveway and turned the car off. "Of the lust part, anyway. I'm not sure it's exactly a hidden agenda. People can probably tell just by the way I look at you how much I want you."

The way people could tell how happy Kate and Cole made each other just by watching them?

She decided to make the most of her uninhibited state. "I want you, too." Without the engine noise or the music from the radio, could he hear her heart thudding?

He groaned, rubbing a thumb over her bottom lip. "So, what now? If I kiss you, I'm afraid I'll try to drag you into the backseat."

"I think," she said slowly, "that you should walk me to my door."

He nodded, his expression crestfallen. "It would be the gentlemanly thing to do."

"Then I should tell my mom good-night. And sneak out."

"What?"

"I never snuck out during my teenage years like

some of my other friends. Don't you think I'm overdue?"

"Long overdue."

"You're not picking up Tommy until tomorrow?"

"Right, he's staying overnight with Kim and her boyfriend."

"Then maybe I could come over. For a little while," she said shyly. She couldn't stay the night, but she could steal a little more of the present for herself.

Megan didn't think any man had ever scrambled out of the car faster than Will did. She was chuckling when he opened her door. "Afraid I'll change my mind?"

"No." His voice was conspiratorial whisper. "But the sooner I walk you home, the sooner you can sneak out."

EVEN THOUGH MEGAN was a grown woman entitled to make her own decisions, there was still an illicit thrill to tiptoeing out of her house. She'd taken the time to wash off her makeup and brush her teeth, but her ardor for Will hadn't lessened in the moments she'd been away from him. If anything, the brief separation made her impatient for him. For his kisses. For his touch.

Are you sure about this? some prim inner voice asked as she crossed the driveway. *You've never had a one-night stand before.*

Well, there was a first time for everything, and she refused to overthink this. When you had a soul-deep craving for chocolate swirl cheesecake, you didn't sit down with the box and read the nutritional information. You grabbed a fork, dove in and worried about calories later.

He was waiting for her on his front porch, barefoot in his slacks and the unbuttoned tuxedo shirt, looking like a potent female fantasy in the moonlight. They came together wordlessly, kissing each other for long, languid moments until he grated, "A better host would have invited you inside by now."

"Hospitality *is* important," she said solemnly.

Taking her hand, he led her through the house, pausing ever so slightly at the door to his bedroom. She nodded.

Then they fell across his bed, kissing again and tugging at each other's clothing so that they could touch each other as intimately as they'd wanted to all evening. Dancing with him at the reception had been fun, but it had also been an exercise in frustration. As much as she'd enjoyed the feel of his muscles beneath the tuxedo, she'd craved the contact of his skin against hers. And Will was more than satisfying those cravings now. Clothes hit the floor so fast that she didn't even have time to feel self-conscious—a blessing after having been pregnant with three babies.

Will, on the other hand, was damn near physical perfection. The hard planes of his torso, silvery in the moonlight, would haunt her most erotic dreams. Intense need built in her as he kissed the hollow of her throat and then her breasts. But she got nervous when he moved lower. He pressed a kiss against the inside of her thigh, and she trembled.

"Wh-what are you doing?"

He grinned at her. "Do you want me to answer that question, or would you rather I just show you?"

She bit her lip. "Wait. I don't think—"

"Megan, so much of your life is lived for other people. Be selfish just this once. Let me do this for you." He stroked his fingers over her in a silky tease, then slid one inside her. "Your job is to enjoy it. Can you do that?"

"Yes." She arched under the heat of his mouth. "Oh yes." Sensation overpowered her, reality seeming to blur as her body tightened with raw, unyielding pleasure. Her orgasm wrung a breathless scream from her, and she was still quivering when Will rolled on a condom and surged inside her.

She cried out again as they rocked together, and he took her mouth in a deep kiss that matched the rhythm of their bodies. He reached down between them, stroking her, and her second climax of the night pulsed through her.

Afterward, Will held her for a long time. She knew she had to leave, but she was too boneless with satisfaction to move.

"I have to go," she said, dotting his forearm with light kisses. "Don't want to get busted being out after curfew."

His soft chuckle was a vibration against her body. "Right. I'd hate for you to get grounded because of me. I'll walk you home as soon as I find the energy to put on pants."

"You don't have to. At least one of us should get to lie here and bask."

"Megan Rivers, I am not letting you walk home alone at this hour no matter how close you live. Besides, I'm hoping to steal another kiss at your front door."

He did exactly that ten minutes later, standing beneath her porch light. He gave her lazy, sweet, dream-of-me kisses. She sighed happily as she returned them.

Tucking her hair behind her ear he asked, "When does your mom leave?"

"Tomorrow afternoon. Dagmar is coming over for lunch, so it will be sometime after that."

He was quiet for a moment. "My work schedule is a little crazy this week—"

She braced herself, waiting to be told that he wouldn't have much time for her.

"—and I'm sure that with Christmas next weekend, your schedule will be hectic, too. But maybe we could spend at least one evening together? I could pick up dinner or we could watch a movie with the girls or see those lights over at Brody's ranch."

"All of those would be good," she said, trying to sound casually agreeable and not breathlessly euphoric. If he was asking her out again, this was definitely not a one-night stand.

Then what is it? A relationship? Neighbors with benefits? She didn't know yet. But, so far, it was making her happier than she'd been in a long damn time.

Chapter Twelve

"…so Sierra and I decided to bury the body behind the barn and start up a new life in Mexico."

Will blinked, realizing that at some point his friend had stopped talking about livestock breeding programs. "What?"

"Oh, good." Jarrett tipped back his cowboy hat. "You've rejoined the conversation."

"Sorry," Will mumbled. When he'd agreed to come to the ranch today and help Jarrett repair fencing, he hadn't known Tommy would keep him up the night before. The kid was cutting his first tooth, which had led to a lot of drooling. And a *lot* of crying. When he'd left the baby up at the ranch house for Jarrett's sister to watch, Will had felt equal parts relieved by the break and guilty for inflicting the teething child on someone else. But Vicki Ross was tough. She'd assured him that, if she could learn to walk again after months in a wheelchair, she could handle a fussy infant for a couple of hours.

"Sure you're up for this?" Jarrett asked, pausing before swinging the hammer toward the post Will held steady. "I understand if you need to go. You look rough."

"I'll survive. Tommy and I are going to Megan's

for dinner, and she has a way with him. She— What?"
He narrowed his eyes at his friend's smirk.

"The two of you made a *very* cute couple at your
brother's wedding."

"Did you just call me cute? Let me see that hammer a minute."

"Admit it, you're crazy about her."

"I don't know what I am." It did seem crazy that he
was so excited about seeing her tonight even though
they probably wouldn't have any real alone time, not
with four kids under four. He'd be lucky if he got to
steal a single kiss. And maybe it was a little crazy that
he was spending all his free time with a woman who
represented everything he wanted to postpone—family,
commitment, permanence. They were even planning to
go to Christmas Eve service together later this week.

Jarrett regarded him knowingly. "Do you remember when Sierra first came to Cupid's Bow?"

"I remember that *you* crashed our one and only date."

"I spent a lot of time fighting my feelings when it
would have been better for everyone involved if I'd
owned up to them sooner."

"I'm not 'fighting' anything. I love being with
Megan, and she knows that. But her life is complicated. And, until Amy comes back, so is mine.
I barely had two solid hours of sleep last night and
you want me to analyze my emotions?" He gave his
friend a look of disgust. "Shut up and swing the damn
hammer, already."

MEGAN COULDN'T BELIEVE that it was already Christmas Eve. *Where did December go?* It had been a
memorable month, full of surprises.

Her daughters did not share her bemusement. They were so full of excitement that they were practically ricocheting off the walls. The only way she got them to sit still long enough to dress them and fix their hair for church tonight was to suggest that it might not be too late for Santa to change his mind about who was on the naughty list. While she'd privately thought that the matching, lacy green Christmas dresses her mother had bought the triplets were a little impractical, Megan had to admit that her daughters looked great. Lily had a white bow in her hair, gleaming against her dark curls, and Daisy had a bright red one. Megan was still trying to situate a sparkly silver bow on Iris's head when the doorbell rang. The rich, melodious tones pealing through the house made her smile; fixing the doorbell was just one of the many wonderful things Will had done for her.

She opened the door to find him standing with the car seat in one hand and a red mesh bag in the other. Stretching up on her tiptoes, she kissed his cheek. "Merry Christmas." She had wondered more than once, if she weren't expecting Spencer tomorrow, would Will have invited her and the girls to spend Christmas with his family? And would she have said yes? She adored the Trents, who had all been very welcoming to her, but a shared family holiday seemed like a serious step.

Trying not to overanalyze her own feelings or what was happening between her and Will, she stepped back and said lightly, "Am I running late, or are you very early? I'm not ready yet."

His gaze slid over her in an admiring caress. "What more do you need to do? I don't think it's possible for a woman to be more beautiful than you already are."

She grinned, raising the hem of her red-and-black skirt just enough so that he could see her bare toes. "For starters, I should probably put on shoes."

"We still have plenty of time," he said over the girls' exuberant greetings. "I did come over early. Since I don't think I'll be seeing you tomorrow, I was hoping I could give you and the girls your presents now."

"You didn't have to get us gifts. You've already cleaned the gutters, fixed the doorbell and installed a carbon monoxide detector." Earlier in the week, he'd tested the smoke alarm batteries, looked up reports on her microwave model and practiced a fire drill with the girls that was both serious enough to educate them and lighthearted enough not to give them nightmares.

He tried to look stern, but his eyes were twinkling. "After the *hours* I spent in a crowded mall—"

"Cupid's Bow doesn't have a mall."

"Fine. After the hours I spent in the toy store on Main Street—"

"Hours?"

"Look, woman, do you want your gifts or not?"

She laughed. "As it happens, we have a few small things for you, too." In theory, they could have exchanged gifts after service tonight, but she would already have her hands full trying to get the girls to settle down for bed. Best to get the gift-giving excitement out of the way now.

They all gathered in the living room, and Will unbuckled Tommy from his car seat so that he could scoot around on the floor. "I already let Tommy open one of his gifts, so he could wear it tonight." That explained the long-sleeved onesie drawn to look like a miniature suit, complete with a Christmas tie.

"Very debonair." She eyed Will's dark button-down shirt and black slacks. "You clean up pretty well, too." Seeing him dressed more formally than usual brought back memories of Cole's wedding night, of the night she'd spent in Will's arms. Longing trembled through her.

Luckily, her daughters were there to play chaperone, interrupting before Megan's desire got out of hand. "Mr. Will! I made this for you." Daisy thrust a gift bag toward him. "Open! Open!" Lily and Iris were tripping over each other, both trying to deliver their presents, as well.

"Hold on. How about we let Mr. Will sit down first?" Glad for the excuse to touch him, she took Will's hand and led him to the sofa. "You girls be careful not to step on baby Tommy."

In somewhat orderly fashion—or as close as they were going to get with Christmas only hours away—the girls lined up their gifts at Will's feet. Before he'd even finished opening Daisy's, she instructed, "Eat it! It's yummy." On the plate inside the bag, she'd arranged a graham cracker fire engine with cookie wheels, a red licorice ladder and a gumdrop siren.

"If she says it's yummy, she knows what she's talking about," Megan said. "She did a lot of taste-testing during this project."

Daisy was already crawling into his lap. "Do you like it, Mr. Will? The gumdrop is my favorite. Gumdrops are yummy." She eyed the edible fire truck pointedly, and Will laughed.

"I *love* my present," he assured her. "But somehow I don't think it's going to last long."

"Open mine!" Iris instructed, climbing onto the couch and wiggling in next to her sister.

Her gift was an art project they'd created by covering her entire hand with red finger paint. She'd made a handprint on paper, then she'd drawn hats and faces on each finger so that it looked like five firemen working together to operate a hose.

"This is wonderful," Will said to her with a hug. "I'm going to ask the captain if we can hang this up at the station." Then he moved on to Lily's gift.

She was watching with wide eyes and her thumb in her mouth. "Faw the Cwistmas twee."

Megan had helped her daughter make an ornament out of clay. It was a firefighter's hat that Lily had painted red; Megan had carefully written Will's last name and number on it. He looked genuinely touched as he thanked the little girl. Lily shifted from foot to foot as if considering coming closer for a snuggle, like her sisters had. She compromised by taking a few steps closer, then sitting on the floor.

"I have a gift for you, too," Megan said, "but compared to what the girls did, it's a little lame." Every time she'd tried to think about what to get Will, she'd faltered. All of her ideas had either seemed too generic for a man who'd seen her naked or too personal, implying too much of a connection or future. Will had made it clear that he didn't want to get too serious about anyone right now, and she didn't want him to feel pressured.

Are you really respecting his feelings? Or are your protecting your own? As long as she told herself that she wasn't too seriously involved, that she wasn't in over her head, maybe she could keep from getting hurt.

Will opened the envelope she'd handed him and grinned at the Smoky Pig gift certificate. "There is *never* anything lame about giving a Texas man the gift of barbecue." He reached past Iris to get the mesh bag from the end table. "Now it's my turn to pass out presents!" He gave the girls three identically wrapped, lumpy packages with uneven seams and too much tape. The extra adhesive didn't slow down the triplets as they tore into the paper.

Shouts of joy echoed through the living room, and all of Megan's daughters were talking at once. "Look, Mama!"

"It's *so cute.*"

"Thank you, Mistah Will." Lily was cuddling an oversize stuffed dog; from the look on her face, it was clear her new best friend would be riding with them to church and no doubt sleeping next to her tonight.

Iris held an adorable plush snowman, and Will reached over to ruffle her curls. "Like you said, Christmas should have snow." Iris nodded emphatically.

He'd done an excellent job shopping for her girls, but it was the stuffed animal Daisy was snuggling that was pure genius. Will had bought her a snarling green T. rex; he'd tied an incongruous purple bow, Daisy's favorite color, around its neck.

"Heads up." Will tossed a lumpy package in Megan's direction, his expression mischievous. "I have one for you, too."

When Megan unwrapped the adorable stuffed hedgehog, she laughed out loud.

Will winked at her. "Merry Christmas, Prickly. Oh, and I almost forgot…" He fished a smaller, professionally wrapped box out of the bag and stood to give it to her.

Inside was a beautiful silver bracelet with three charms depicting a daisy, a lily and an iris. Tears pricked her eyes. "This is gorgeous. Help me put it on?" With a couple of tries, she could've managed it herself, but she ached for the physical contact. He fastened the delicate chain around her wrist, then surreptitiously pressed a kiss to her palm while the girls were distracted "introducing" their new stuffed animals to each other. Afterward, Megan made Tommy a bottle to take with them while Will and the girls snacked on licorice and cookies. There was a lot of giggling and chattering as everyone climbed into the van, full of sugar and holiday spirit.

The parking lot of the church was packed, and by the time they dropped off the girls and Tommy in their age-respective nursery rooms, Megan could hear the strains of music that signaled service was starting. She walked faster toward the staircase that led up to the sanctuary.

"Rats," she muttered, "we're late."

Will took her hand. "Don't worry, Kate and Cole are saving us seats. And since we're late already…" He surprised her by lightly pressing her against the wall and stealing a brief but thorough kiss.

When he released her, she was breathless. "I'm not sure you're supposed to do that here."

"I thank God for bringing you into my life, and I'd

like to think He wouldn't mind my expressing appreciation." He gave her a boyish grin. "Now, come on, slowpoke, or we won't make it before the final hymn."

Fingers laced together, both wearing matching smiles, they hurried up the steps. He slipped into the sanctuary while the congregation was standing to sing "O Come, All Ye Faithful." The Trent family all squished closer together to make room for Megan and Will in the pew. Kate flashed her a smile that was both welcoming and perceptive, as if she somehow knew about the stolen kiss. Megan darted a glance toward Will to make sure none of her lipstick was on him. Last Christmas, she'd been the mother of two-year-olds, packing to move into a new house. She'd been so tired she barely had the energy to wrap gifts, simply shoving toys into red and green bags. But now here she was, in a new town and a new life, happier than she would've believed possible.

Life felt almost too good to be true, which made the cautious divorcée in her nervous.

"Everything okay?" Will whispered.

She blinked. Everyone around her was standing for fellowship greeting, shaking hands and exchanging hugs. Megan hadn't even realized it was time to rise. Belatedly, she stood. "Fine." After that, she forced herself to push away her doubts and focus on the adorable Nativity pageant being performed by five-, six- and seven-year-olds. One of Cole's daughters was an angel, the other was a sheep who kept *baa*-ing with gusto. Finally, service concluded with every member of the congregation lighting a candle and singing an a cappella version of "Silent Night." The simple beauty of the moment made Megan feel weepy.

Rather than rush immediately for the exit once service was finished, Will's family waited for the crowd to thin out. Megan took the opportunity to say hello to each of the Trents, since she'd come in too late to chat with them before church started.

Will's father surprised her with a large bear hug. "Wish you could join us tomorrow. Your presence would be an added touch of class."

Gayle raised an eyebrow. "Are you saying I don't keep a dignified home?"

He laughed. "I'm saying we need all the help we can get to counterbalance Jace."

"Hey!" Will's younger brother objected.

Cole gave him a reproving look. "You once tried to burp 'Deck the Halls.'"

"I was a teenager."

"It was a week before your twentieth birthday."

"Nineteen is a teenager."

Megan chuckled at their brotherly gibing. Christmas at the Trent house sounded, if possible, even more lively than Christmas with the triplets. *Speaking of which…* "I'd better hurry to the nursery." Now that other parents were starting to pick up their kids, her daughters were probably getting antsy to go home and put out cookies for Santa.

Will told his family he would see them all the next day, then headed for a side door. It wasn't easy to keep up with his long-legged stride.

"Are you trying to ditch me?" she teased.

He immediately slowed, flashing her an apologetic grin. "Hey, you're the one who said we needed to hurry."

"I meant more of a moderate hurry. Less emergency building evacuation, more spirited amble."

He laughed as they rounded the corner to the three-year-old nursery room. Lily, coloring a picture just inside the door, glanced up at the sound. A huge grin spread across her face, her expression as bright as Christmas morning. "Mistah Will!" Her crayon fell to the floor as she ran toward him, arms outstretched and hair bow crooked.

He automatically knelt down to catch her, wrapping her in his strong arms. Suddenly, Megan couldn't breathe past the lump in her throat. Noticing the commotion, Daisy and Iris came running, too. Will folded them all into a group hug. Even though Lily was already squirming away to retrieve her stuffed dog and her picture, the fact remained that Megan's reserved daughter had sprinted toward Will with the kind of unrestrained adoration she'd only shown for a handful of people in her life. The triplets loved him.

And so do I.

Maybe, under much different circumstances, she would've felt joy at the revelation. But all of her emotional resources were currently tied up trying to stave off blind panic. Will Trent was a wonderful man, perhaps even the best one she'd ever met. But he wanted his bachelor freedom, had talked about dodging the bullet of serious commitment. She already had a failed marriage behind her in which she'd been more invested in the relationship than the man who'd sworn to love her; she wouldn't set herself up for that kind of hurt again.

Worse, she wasn't the only one who stood to get hurt. Her mother's warnings echoed in her ears.

Megan had daughters to look after, to shield from pain. They were already so attached to him, more excited about Will's visits than seeing their own father tomorrow. How devastated would they be when Megan scared Will off by getting too serious, too fast?

I'm supposed to protect them.

She should have done a better job protecting her heart. Instead, whether he knew it or not, she'd handed it over to Will, just as heedlessly as Lily had barreled into his arms.

WILL EXCHANGED NODS with people he'd known all his life, seeing the amusement on some of their faces at the sight of him carrying a baby and surrounded by preschoolers. *If anyone had told me a month ago, I never would've believed them.* Even now he suspected that the reason he didn't feel more self-conscious was because the situation was temporary. He cared a lot about Tommy, would be willing to risk his own life to save the baby's, but that didn't mean he was ready to *have* a baby.

Still, the thought of someday building a family no longer seemed as far-fetched as it had in recent months.

Once they reached the parking lot, Megan handed him the keys. "Do you mind driving? I...have a bit of a headache."

That explained how preoccupied she'd seemed during the church service and the pained expression on her face as they exited the building. With the girls chattering, it was easy to miss how quiet Megan had become, but he'd started to wonder if something was bothering her.

"Of course I'll drive." Maybe when they got back to her place, he could make her a cup of tea or help her get the girls ready for bed.

He'd always liked the triplets; they reminded him of his beloved nieces. But for a moment back there, when little Lily had tackle-hugged him, his usual affection had amplified into something even more powerful and poignant. He suddenly realized that even though he'd brought their Christmas presents over tonight, his holiday tomorrow wouldn't feel complete if he didn't see them.

That's you being selfish. The girls almost never got to spend time with their father, and Will didn't have any right to interrupt their family holiday. But Megan had mentioned that Spencer was staying in a hotel, so maybe if Will waited until—

"You aren't expecting your ex tonight, are you?" Will squinted at the car parked in their driveway. It was difficult to tell in the dark, but he didn't think it belonged to anyone he knew.

"Definitely not." Megan straightened in her seat, her expression alarmed, as if she couldn't bear the thought of dealing with Spencer right now. "That doesn't look like his car. Although I suppose it could be Bonnie's."

As Will turned into the driveway, he spotted a figure on his front porch. He did a double take, not believing his eyes at first. "It's Amy."

She rushed down to meet them, seeming to vibrate with nervous energy as she waited for him to open his door. She looked as if she'd gained a few healthy pounds in the last few weeks, no longer gaunt. Her expression was anxious, but her gaze was bright and alert. He hadn't realized until just then how accustomed he'd become to the glazed look of defeat in her eyes.

Happy for her and for the progress she'd made, he enveloped her in a heartfelt hug. "Welcome back! I wish I'd known you were coming. I would've left you a key, instead of you sitting out in the cold."

"I barely felt it. I was too excited about seeing Tommy again." Her voice broke a little as she said her son's name. "I know I still have work to do in rehab, but I just could not miss his first Christmas."

The girls were piling out of the van now, demanding to know who Amy was.

"This is Tommy's mama," Megan explained, "and we should go inside so that she and Mr. Will can talk."

Amy rounded the car to hug Megan, too. "Will said you helped take care of my son. *Thank you.*" Tears were starting to spill, and Will tried to catch Megan's eye, to signal that she should stay. He wasn't great with crying females.

Case in point, last time he'd had a crying woman in his house, she'd fled, leaving him with a baby for three weeks.

"Don't mention it," Megan said gently. "He's a sweetie pie."

Will had reached into the car to unbuckle Tommy from his seat. Should he tell Amy that the baby was crawling now, or just let her see for herself? They should also talk about Dr. Ingram adding cereal to Tommy's diet. "Here." He turned to Amy. "There's someone who I'm sure would very much like to see you."

Cradling her son against her, Amy burst into full-fledged sobs.

Casting a sympathetic glance in the younger woman's direction, Megan told Will, "Take that girl inside and get her a glass of water and a box of tissues. Maybe some hot chocolate, if you have any."

He nodded. "I'm so glad she's back." If she had missed her son's first Christmas, he doubted she ever would have forgiven herself, even if Tommy was too young to remember it later.

"I'll bet. Your life is finally yours again."

He grinned at that, pleased by the prospect of not being covered in cereal or having to change diapers at four in the morning. "Just in the nick of time." His place was barely baby-proofed enough for crawling; he couldn't imagine how much trickier parenting would become once Tommy attempted to walk.

Megan's expression was pained, and his relief at Amy's return momentarily took a backseat to concern. Her headache was obviously getting worse. "Are you going to be okay? I can come over after Amy leaves if you need—"

"I can take care of myself."

It was the prickliest she'd sounded in weeks, and he couldn't help wondering if her crankiness was due solely to a throbbing skull. He'd almost detected... anger?

"Megan, did I do something wrong?"

"No." She shook her head sadly. "No, you are not the problem. Now go, get that girl inside. The two of you have a lot to discuss."

He pressed a light kiss to her forehead and turned to do as she suggested. But as he ushered Amy into the house, he couldn't help wondering if there was also a conversation he and Megan needed to have.

AFTER THE INITIAL waterworks had passed, Amy pulled herself together pretty quickly. At first they talked at the kitchen table, where this had all started, and she told him about her rehabilitation program and how wonderful her aunt Nadine had been. But they soon moved to the living room floor, where Tommy could crawl around on the carpet with fewer obstacles.

Amy sniffed. "I can't believe I wasn't here when he started crawling."

"It's good that you got yourself off a self-destructive path. If you'd continued down that road, you might've missed so many more milestones. You still have a lot to look forward to—first steps, first words." He gave her an evil grin. "Potty training."

She laughed. "I missed him so much that, right now, even that sounds good."

"Maybe there are ways to reduce your work hours so that you don't miss so many moments. I was serious when I said my mother is willing to help you investigate new job possibilities."

She leaned against the side of the sofa, her expression one of bewilderment. "I can't get over how kind everyone in your family is. The world would be a different place if more people were like the Trents. But as much as I truly appreciate the offer, I don't think I'm ready to come home to Cupid's Bow just yet. Aunt Nadine is staying at the hotel out by the hospital—that's her car I'm driving. She said mine wasn't roadworthy."

"She's right," Will said, recalling the junk heap Amy had been driving last time he saw her.

"Anyway, she and I are going to spend tomorrow with my mother, since it's Christmas. Then I think Tommy and I will stay with Nadine for a few months. I didn't see her very often when I was younger, because of her drug problems, but now that she's cleaned up, she is a bona fide godsend. If I'd realized a month ago how wonderful she is, I probably would've taken Tommy with me and spared you all the hassle. I'm sorry."

"I'm not." He wasn't just saying that to make Amy feel better, either. If Tommy hadn't been here, if Will hadn't so desperately needed help, he never would've knocked on his neighbor's door. How would he and Megan have gotten to know each other? Or would they have remained strangers? That was a horrible thought. In a matter of weeks, she'd become one of the most important people in his life.

Without knowing it, by leaving Tommy here, Amy had given him an amazing Christmas gift—Megan Rivers and her adorable triplets.

Amy's phone chirped a text alert, and she glanced down at the screen. She had pulled the phone out of her pocket earlier, and by Will's count, she'd taken nine thousand pictures of Tommy since stepping into the house. "Aunt Nadine is worried about me. I guess it is starting to get late."

"Are you okay to drive?" He knew it had been an emotional night for her.

"Will, I am the best I have been in months."

He believed her. "If you give me the keys to your car, I'll go set up Tommy's seat and you can have a few more minutes to play with him."

"And change his diaper." She grimaced. "He smells a little ripe."

"I will sincerely miss the little guy—you'd better visit me—but I will not miss diaper duty. Ever."

EVEN THOUGH SOME of Tommy's stuff was still there—Amy had said either she or her aunt would pick up the rest of it after Christmas—Will's house felt bizarrely empty after she drove away. A couple of hours ago, he'd been in a noisy van with five other people. Now he was alone.

As the quiet settled around him, his thoughts turned back to Megan. Actually, that wasn't quite true. She'd stayed on his mind all night, even as he'd been listening to Amy. Selfishly, he wanted to talk to Megan, see her. But what if she was asleep? Going to bed would probably be the best remedy for her headache.

Then again, it was Christmas Eve. According to his older brother, this was the night thousands of parents stayed awake to assemble presents and curse toy manufacturers. One of Cole's more entertaining tall tales was the dramatic reenactment he did of the hours it had taken to cut free a baby doll stroller from its insane packaging and put it together.

Maybe Megan could use a hand. Maybe she would enjoy some company.

He knew he couldn't stay the night, not with the girls as witnesses, but he'd love to be with her when Christmas Day officially arrived. Locking the door behind him, he stepped out on his front porch and texted Megan. You awake?

When three dots immediately appeared to show she was typing a response, he hit the call button.

"I was just texting you back," she said as she answered.

"I know. But hearing your voice is even better." There was a long pause that halted him midway across her yard. "Megan? How's your headache?"

"Now that the girls are asleep, it's manageable."

"Good. Amy's gone. I truly believe she and Tommy are going to be okay."

"I'm relieved to hear that. She's lucky to have you in her life."

"And I'm lucky to have you. I couldn't have taken care of him by myself. These last few weeks have put me in awe of single parents. I don't know how you do it, Megan."

"One day at a time." She sounded sad.

Whatever the problem was, he desperately wanted to fix it. "My brother Cole has told stories about the woes of assembling last-minute toys on Christmas Eve. I thought maybe I could come over and help."

"Thanks, but luckily they wanted a lot of art supplies. Not too much assembling required. I was just curled up on the sofa watching the end of a Bing Crosby movie."

"Then maybe I could watch that with you. I give excellent foot rubs."

"Thanks, but the credits are rolling."

He sighed. Why did conversation with her suddenly feel difficult? Because it was over the phone and not in person? "Then maybe we could just talk."

"You have a lot to process," she said.

I do?

"We can talk after Christmas."

"Or now, since I'm standing in your front yard." He'd been waiting for her to officially invite him over before he volunteered that, but since an invitation didn't seem to be forthcoming… "You should probably let me in before Abe Martin across the street mistakes me for a prowler and call the cops."

"Probably." The call disconnected, and a moment later, he heard the locks. She opened the door, her hair rumpled and backlit from the kitchen. She was wearing a battered robe over Christmas pajamas and was easily the most gorgeous woman he'd ever seen. Even with her melancholy expression.

"You look like you're worried you won't get what you wanted for Christmas," he said lightly. "Want me to put in a last-minute word for you with Santa?"

The corner of her mouth turned up in a wistful smile. "Bringing your brother over here to play Santa was such a nice thing to do for the girls. You've done more nice things for them, for me, than I can count. And I don't want you to think I'm ungrateful, but…"

A horrible pressure tightened in his chest. "But what?"

"I was already starting to wonder if we've been spending too much time together. And—"

"You have?" Because he'd been having pretty much the opposite reaction. The more time he spent with Megan, the more he thought about her, the more he *wanted* to be with her.

She gave him a look that was affectionately pitying, one that reminded him uncomfortably of an expression he'd seen before. On Tasha's face, the night before their wedding. *Oh God, not again.*

"We've been thrown together by circumstances," Megan said, her voice starting to shake, "and it's easy to get confused. Especially if you're three years old. Tomorrow, Spencer is going to tell the girls that he's remarrying. I don't want them getting the wrong idea about you and me just because we've been spending so much time together. Distance would be good for all of us."

"I disagree," he said quietly. "If they got the idea that I cared about you, that I cared about them, it wouldn't be the wrong one." Jarrett had been right— best to face his feelings head-on and let Megan know how much she meant to him. "I'm falling—"

"Please don't!" She shook her head, wild-eyed. "With Tommy gone, you just got your life back. Your freedom. The Christmas season is nostalgic and sentimental, but that doesn't last. I don't want you to realize a month from now you've made a horrible mistake. We've had a great time, but I think it's come to its natural end. I hope we—"

"Do not ask if we can be friends," he interrupted, nauseated with déjà vu. He was furious. Furious with her for this emotional sucker punch, and furious that he'd allowed himself to fall for someone again with no better results than the first time. *You'd think I would learn.* It took effort to speak, his throat was so raw with emotions. "Is this really what you want, Megan?"

Her eyes glittered. "It makes the most sense. You can resume making up for lost dating time, and I can focus on my girls and help them adjust to the idea of a stepmom."

"But is it what you *want*?" He took a step closer, half tempted to try to kiss sense into her.

"Yes." Her voice was a broken whisper.

He knew she was lying—they both knew it—but as she pulled away and closed the front door between them, he also knew he couldn't coerce her to give them a future. With Tasha, he'd tried for hours, talking until he was blue in the face, suggesting they postpone the wedding instead of canceling it out right. Nothing he had said had changed her mind.

At least this time, he was walking away with his dignity intact.

Chapter Thirteen

In an excited rush to get to their Christmas presents, the triplets were up at dawn. Normally, this would have been difficult for Megan, but since she'd spent a sleepless night second-guessing herself and her taste in men, three hyper girls were a nice distraction. For the two hours that it took them to open their gifts and ooh and aah over the contents of their stockings, Megan managed to keep most of her focus on her daughters. She doled out smiles and hugs and hot cocoa that was 90 percent melted marshmallow. But as the time drew closer for Spencer to arrive, her mood soured.

She got the girls dressed and cleaned up the shredded wrapping paper that decorated her living room like confetti. Then she considered her own clothing options. Frankly, she would just as soon spend the whole day in her robe. Then again, there was a sliver of female vanity that insisted she put on a good face in front of her ex and the new woman in his life. She pulled on a pair of jeans and a festive Christmas sweater that felt ironic in her current frame of mind, then brushed her hair until it shone. She was securing it into a high, bouncy ponytail when the recently repaired doorbell rang. She winced, immediately thinking of Will as she made her way to the front of the house.

And that is the last thought you spare him for the rest of the day, she chastised herself. After all, ending things had been her idea. She needed to own her decision and move forward, confident that she was doing the right thing for herself and her daughters. It was so tempting to believe that Will might really love her, that his feelings would continue past the rose-colored Christmas season even though he no longer needed her help with Tommy. She wanted to give him—wanted to give them—the benefit of the doubt. Just as she'd given Spencer the benefit of the doubt when she listened to him instead of her own instincts, taking his word for it that there was no affair. After her worst suspicions had proven true, and he'd tearfully told her that it was a onetime panicked reaction to learning they were about to have not just one baby but three, she'd given him the benefit of the doubt again. And had been burned.

How foolish would she be not to trust her instincts now, to take a man's word over what she felt was true? She knew Will cared about her, but she came as a package deal. How long would it take before he resented the loss of his freedom, before he balked at the responsibility of three little girls? *I can't take that chance.*

The doorbell sounded again, this time accompanied by Spencer's voice. "Megan?"

Oops. She hadn't realized that she'd stopped dead in the foyer, no longer making any progress toward the door. But she forced herself to reach for the knob, pasting a big smile on her face. "Merry Christmas," she said as she swung the door open.

There stood Spencer, looking exactly the same as he had the last time she'd seen him, right down to what she was pretty sure was the same tie. Honestly, who wore a suit to spend Christmas morning with his children? She turned her attention from him to the woman at his side, trying not to gape in surprise. "You, um, you must be Bonnie."

Like Megan, the woman had long, dark hair and light eyes. Her height and shape were roughly the same as Megan's, too. *He definitely has a type.* She heard Will's voice in her head. *I'm partial to brunettes.*

Dammit, so much for her vow not to think about Will. She scowled. Then, realizing that Spencer and Bonnie were staring at her, forced her features back into a smile. "Come in, come in. The girls are excited to see you both." She'd debated telling the girls about the engagement, so that they had time to get used to the idea and didn't startle their father with any meltdowns. In the end, however, she'd decided against it. Not only wasn't the engagement her news to share, they'd never even met Bonnie. She had decided it would be less traumatic if they could see she was a kind, normal person; based on the evil stepmothers prevalent in animated fairy tales, they might imagine the worst. Also, since Spencer was not the most reliable man on the planet, Megan wanted to make sure that he actually went through with the proposal— and that Bonnie accepted—before anyone potentially upset the triplets.

"Here, let me help you with those." She reached out to give them a hand with the tower of presents they carried, trying to sneak a glance at Bonnie's ring finger. Sure enough, a diamond engagement ring glittered there. It was funny how numb Megan was at the sight. She would've expected to feel more upset, more betrayed, more wistful for what-might've-been. But she was so emotionally wrung out over Will that her only response was a mental shrug. *I hope Bonnie knows what she's getting into. And I hope Spencer does better this time around.*

In a low voice, she said to them, "Looks like congratulations are in order. I have a bottle of champagne in the back of the fridge we can open later. It's cheap, but sincere."

Bonnie's eyes widened. "Thank you. That's unbelievably kind."

"My pleasure." Maybe this day would be easier with a glass of alcohol. But as much she wanted to believe it, she doubted anything would make this day easier. Or the next day, or the one after that. She'd dealt with a broken heart before, and she knew it would take lots and lots of time.

She just had to take comfort in the fact that she'd ended things with Will before they got any more serious and her daughters' hearts were broken, too.

WILL'S GOAL HAD been to make it through Christmas dinner; if he could make it that long, then he could excuse himself to go home without suffocating guilt. Traditionally, there was a Christmas-themed game night after the table was cleared and the kitchen cleaned, but he knew he was lousy company. The only saving grace was that everybody was so distracted— the kids with presents, Kate and Cole with each other, his parents with maintaining order—he doubted anyone had noticed.

As it turned out, he was wrong. But then, that was becoming a pattern.

"What gives?" Jace asked out of the side of his mouth.

"What are you talking about?" Will paid heavy attention to the glass pan he was scrubbing, not meeting his brother's gaze. "And why are you talking like an old-school movie mobster?"

Jace set down the plates he'd been carrying and folded his arms across his chest. "I was *trying* to be discreet. I figured that if you haven't mentioned by now what's wrong, then you don't want everyone to know."

"What makes you think I want you to know?"

Jace studied him for a long minute. "It's Megan, isn't it?"

He flinched at the sound of her name, gritting his teeth against the onslaught of pain that accompanied it. Her voice echoed in his head, taunting, telling him that their relationship had reached its natural end. *What a load of crap.*

"I'll take that as a yes," Jace said. "Man, I was hoping to be wrong. But she made you happier than I've seen you in a long time, so it stood to reason that maybe she is what's making you so miserable."

"I really don't want to talk about this."

"Talk about what?" Cole asked as he carried in two tumblers and set about refilling them with iced tea.

"Will and Megan got into a fight."

"It wasn't a fight."

"What did you do wrong?" Cole asked.

Will glared. "What the hell kind of brotherly support is that?"

"Arguably more supportive than you were," Cole said. "Do you happen to recall when Kate and I first started to get serious and she was tentative about being involved with a cop? *Your* supportive words of wisdom included something about how if there was an obstacle in the road, maybe it was better to avoid the road altogether."

Heat crept up his neck. "Sorry about that," he mumbled. "I just didn't want to see you get hurt." The way Will had been hurt before, the way he was hurting again now.

"Understood." Cole clapped him on the back. "So what did you do wrong?"

Will balled his hands into fists. *Not a damn thing.* He'd been attentive, passionate, thoughtful. Admiring of her skills as a mother, kind to her children. Yet none of it had been enough. "The only thing I did wrong was fall for another woman without the good sense to appreciate me."

THE DAY AFTER CHRISTMAS, her daughters gave Megan the best gift possible—a quiet morning. After all the excitement yesterday, they slept well past nine on Monday, and she decided not to wake them up. Forget organized schedules and keeping the girls on track, knowing she'd need to wake them up early again tomorrow; right now she needed the peace.

So, naturally, her mother called two minutes after Megan sat down to enjoy her chai tea.

Megan reached for the phone grudgingly but unwilling to let it keep ringing, for fear it might wake the girls. "Hello?" she asked, her voice barely above a whisper.

"Megan? Are you sick, dear? Your throat sounds scratchy."

Yes, say you're sick. Maybe she'll let you hang up without a massive guilt trip. Then again, a lie could backfire horribly, if her mother showed up for another surprise visit, determined to nurse her back to health. "I'm fine." Funny how that felt more like a lie than saying she was sick.

"I left you a voice mail yesterday, to wish you and the girls a merry Christmas."

"I know, thanks. I heard it right before I went to bed. I was planning to call you later, when the girls are up and can tell you about their presents from Santa. Yesterday was crazy with Spencer here."

"And that woman? Did he actually bring her?" her mother asked disdainfully.

"Bonnie. She seemed nice enough." Megan didn't bear the woman any ill will. "As far as I know, he met her a few months ago. She had nothing to do with our marriage ending, and she was friendly to the kids. Daisy and Iris really liked her. Lily mostly hid in the corner behind the rocking chair, eyeing her skeptically, but that was her reaction to Spencer, too." He'd been humiliated that he had so much trouble coaxing out his own child in front of his fiancée. Megan had empathized, but she refused to force Lily to interact with virtual strangers. If Spencer wanted to be treated like a beloved daddy, he needed to start acting like one.

"Is he still in town?"

"They were planning to leave this morning and spend a few days with Bonnie's mom in Oklahoma."

As it turned out, when Spencer had said they were spending Christmas with Bonnie's parents, he'd meant her father and stepmother, who'd primarily raised her. It was her background as the child of divorce, she'd told Megan, that made her understand how important it was for Spencer to maintain a relationship with his children, for all the adults in the situation to behave cordially. Apparently, it was only in the last few years that her own parents had been able to enter the same room without screaming at each other.

"I think Bonnie might actually be good for him," Megan said.

"And have you given any more thought to what's good for you and the girls?"

"You're talking about Will?" She did not want to discuss this. But why not get it over with so that she didn't have to endure any more well-intentioned, unsolicited advice? "Actually, he and I are no longer seeing each other."

"Honey, I'm *so* sorry. But I did try to warn you. You have three daughters. You can't be surprised that a man like him—"

"I broke up with him, Mother, not the other way around."

"Oh." That shut her up.

They sat in awkward silence, Megan sipping the tea that had started to grow cold.

Finally, Beth Ann offered, "I think being involved with him would be a mistake—I've made no secret of that—but I'm truly sorry for any interim pain. All

I wish for you is happiness. I didn't want to see you get hurt again."

"Neither did I." *And yet here I am.*

AT THE UNEXPECTED knock on his front door, hope rushed through Will. Maybe Megan had changed her mind? He knew from experience that she was unafraid to admit when she was wrong, one of her brave qualities, and if she'd missed him the last two days half as much as he'd missed her...

He hustled to the door, banging his shin on a table and stubbing a toe along the way. But he knew any pain would fade at the sight of her face. Unfortunately, the woman on his front porch was a pretty blonde he'd never seen before in his life.

"Can I help you?" Maybe she was visiting relatives for the holidays and had shown up at the wrong house by mistake.

She gave him an appraising look. "Are you Will Trent?"

"Yes, ma'am."

"Nadine Reynolds," she said, grasping his hand in both of hers.

"*You're* Aunt Nadine?" She could hardly be ten years older than Amy. "You're a lot younger than I expected."

Her grin brought out two dimples. "Back at you! The way Amy talked about how 'solid' and 'wise' you are and your experience as a fireman, she made you sound... I hesitate to use the word *fatherly*."

"Please, hesitate. Let's go with big brotherly."

She picked up a gift basket that had been sitting by

her feet. "This is for you. As both a Christmas present and a thank-you. You were a genuine lifesaver."

"She's the one who was willing to admit she needed help and sought it out. I can't take all the credit. I can, however, accept these delicious-looking goodies." He reached for the basket of cheese and sausage and gourmet crackers, trying to look appropriately grateful. But it reminded him of the baskets-in-progress that frequently lined Megan's counters and took up space in her spare bedroom. Refusing to glance toward Megan's house, he ushered Nadine inside before he did something stupid. Like stare next door and sigh longingly at the rain gutters. *She doesn't want you. Have some pride.*

"I hope you don't mind my coming over to gather the last of Tommy's things," Nadine said as he brought an armload of supplies out of his bedroom. "Amy wanted to come herself, but she decided she owed in-person explanations to all of her former employers. So she borrowed her mom's car to run those errands, and I volunteered to take care of this. We'd like to hit the road first thing in the morning."

"Is Tommy with her mother?"

"No." Nadine's smile was rueful. "Amy hasn't let him out of her sight since she came over here Christmas Eve. She missed him so much."

"It's good of you to let them live with you," he said as he glanced around, doing one last sweep for stray teething rings and containers of wet wipes.

"I was screwed up through my teens and twenties and never got married or had children. This is like my second chance at a family. Which I guess doesn't make a lick of sense, since I never had a first chance."

"I knew what you meant," he assured her as he escorted her to the door, both of them carrying Tommy's belongings.

Once they had everything loaded in the trunk of her car, he gave her his phone number. "I know Amy already has it, but I'd like you to have it, too. In case of an emergency, I guess. Or just… Please text me pictures of the little man?" A staggering wave of melancholy hit him. "I miss him."

"Regular reports," she promised. Then she surprised him by throwing her arms around him and squeezing him in a friendly hug. "Thank you so much, Mr. Trent."

"You're wel—" He froze, some sixth sense alerting him that they were being watched. Glancing over Nadine's shoulder, he saw Megan standing just outside her front door, a trash bag in each hand. She looked stricken, eyeing him in the embrace of another woman. "Megan!"

But instead of answering, she pivoted and fled back into the house, garbage bags and all.

He swore under his breath, and Nadine took a nervous step backward. "That was your neighbor Megan? Amy mentioned her, too. Is…everything all right?"

No. And not just because Megan had glimpsed him holding another woman; that was a stupid misunderstanding. The stupid part was that, even after all they'd shared, Megan didn't know him well enough to understand there was no way he could be with someone else two days after she'd kicked him to the curb. Did she truly have no comprehension of what she'd meant to him? Did she really think he was so shallow that he could replace her as easily as batteries in a smoke alarm?

If that's what she thought of him, perhaps it was for the best that she'd set him free. But he was getting damn tired of having to find these silver linings in the aftermath of his wrecked relationships. There were only so many blessings in disguise a guy could take.

"Hey." Kim Jordan snapped her fingers in front of Will's face. "Are you awake, or did you master the elusive art of sleeping with your eyes open?"

He glanced up from the table at the station house, bleary-eyed. "If I were sleeping, I'd look better rested." He'd been on call for two days and was starting to feel it, despite the hours he'd taken in the bunk room.

"Well, you're off shift now. Go home."

"I'm not off shift until Thursday evening."

"Trent, it *is* Thursday evening."

"Oh. Guess I'd better head home, then." Home to his unnaturally quiet house to be alone. He didn't want to be around his family members, who kept trying to give him romantic advice. And he didn't want to date anyone ever again.

Why the hell not? She already thinks you are. Being celibate and miserable wasn't going to change anything.

"Kim, do you want to go out with me?"

She raised an eyebrow. "Just how sleep deprived are you? I have a serious boyfriend."

"Right. I knew that. I was kidding."

"Your sense of humor is getting weirder every day. Go home, get some sleep."

It was sound advice, but even as he gathered his

belongings, he couldn't muster any enthusiasm for returning to his house. Maybe because every time he drove up to it, he also saw *her* house. He took a solemn oath never to date another woman who lived on his street—not that he expected sixty-three-year-old Juliana Baracnik, the only other single female on Wyatt Lane, to make a play for him anytime soon.

Muttering to himself about learning from his mistakes, he almost crashed into someone coming out of the captain's office. When he glanced up to apologize, he found Becca Johnston peering at him.

"Sorry about that," he said.

"Don't worry about me, but are you okay?"

"Maybe more light-headed than I should be. I didn't eat lunch." He wasn't entirely certain he'd eaten breakfast. Although he'd managed a few bites at Christmas to spare his mom's feelings, he hadn't had any real appetite all week. "I'll grab something along Main Street before I drive home. Becca, would you like to have dinner with me?" *She* didn't live in his neighborhood.

Becca was attractive and intelligent, so why had he never asked her out? Possibly because she was a single mother, although that no longer seemed like a deterrent. Or maybe because she used to harbor unrequited feelings for his brother Cole, although that was ancient history. Or, perhaps, Will had never considered dating her because she was widely regarded as terrifying. She was extremely single-minded, but at the moment he found that a refreshing, attractive quality.

"I admire you, Becca. And do you know why? Because you're a take-charge woman who knows her mind." Not someone who waffled, seeming to adore you one day and pushing you out of her life the next. If you screwed up, Becca would let you know—and likely make you pay—but a man would know where he stood with her. There would be no yanking the rug out from under him just when he was comfortable with his life, just when he dared to be *happy* again. "The Smoky Pig's only a block away. How about it?"

"It is difficult to turn down someone who admires my mind and isn't afraid of a strong woman." She made a face. "I've discovered since my divorce that some men in this town are wimps. The rest all seem bitter about my louse of an ex-husband swindling them in real estate fraud. You didn't do any business with him, did you?"

"Nope."

She locked her arm through his. "Then let's get our barbecue on."

"Wonderful." He even had a gift certificate in his wallet to pay for the meal.

HALFWAY THROUGH DINNER, Will was beginning to regret his impulsive invitation. Becca, despite her reputation as a benevolent tyrant, was surprisingly good company. But he discovered that he no longer knew how to behave on a date. After Tasha left, he'd reinvented himself as Will Trent, Ladies' Man. He'd been full of charm and flirtatious patter. That felt meaningless now, and an insult to Becca's intelligence.

Once they'd discussed why she'd been at the station house—to finalize arrangements for on-site firefighters during the town's New Year's Eve fireworks—he had no idea what to say to her. During one particularly awkward lull in conversation, he finally thought to do the obvious and asked her about her son, Marc, who was in elementary school.

Becca glowed with maternal pride as she listed his recent accomplishments, including winter spelling bee champion. She wiped all the barbecue sauce off her fingers so that she could pull out her phone and illustrate her stories with pictures. Before Will knew what he was doing, he'd reached for his own phone to show her the two baby photos Amy had sent yesterday. Once he was scrolling through snapshots, it seemed only natural to show her a picture of the triplets in their Christmas dresses and one he'd taken at the Leonard Tree Farm of Iris "hiding," completely visible behind a skinny pine tree.

When he realized that Becca's responses had become more stilted, he suddenly glanced up to find her regarding him with a combination of annoyance and sympathy. How long had he been talking about Megan and her children? "I'm a terrible date, aren't I?" *What the hell happened to me?* Last month, he'd been great at this. "Instead of getting to know you better, I'm boring you with pictures of kids who aren't even mine."

"I'm not bored. But I am wondering why you asked *me* to dinner," Becca said with her characteristic bluntness, "and not Megan Rivers."

He was at a loss for how to respond; he hadn't expected the topic of Megan to come up on his date. *Then maybe you shouldn't have mentioned her, genius.* "Megan's my next-door neighbor. She's a nice lady, but we're just friends."

"Will." She tilted her head, giving him an exasperated who-are-you-kidding? look. "Everyone from here to Turtle knows about your kiss under the mistletoe. And I was *at* your brother's wedding, remember?"

Oh. Actually, he'd forgotten that. Becca and Kate did lots of community work together, so of course his sister-in-law would have invited her. But he hadn't noticed Becca that night. Probably because he'd been preoccupied with his own date.

"All right," he relented, "there *was* something romantic between me and Megan. But it was short-lived."

"You don't sound happy about that."

Was he ever going to feel happy again? "I just need time. I'll get over her." Like he'd gotten over Tasha.

"Why?"

He stared, unable to make sense of the question. "What do you mean?"

"Why are you trying to get over her instead of trying to get her back?"

How would he win her back? And, more importantly, why should he? *She* had pushed *him* away. "Megan doesn't feel the same way about me that I do about her."

"You don't know what you're talking about, you big dummy."

"Um, Becca? Statements like that are why people find you abrasive."

She waved a hand dismissively. "There are worse things in this world than a little abrasion. Real estate fraud, for one. Quitters, for another."

"I'm not a quitter!" He hadn't meant to say that so loudly. Other diners turned to stare. In a much softer tone, he asked, "Why would you say I don't know what I'm talking about? Do you have some reason to believe Megan has feelings for me?"

"Aside from the obvious adoration on her face at the wedding? I went in her shop yesterday to order some gift baskets as luncheon door prizes, and she looked worse than you do. Shadows under her eyes, no smile for her customers. She looks heartbroken."

Despite an effort to remain indifferent, he felt a small leap of hope. "If she wanted to be with me, why push me away?"

"What explanation did she give you?"

"That she was safeguarding her daughters against an eventual breakup." Which was a load of manure. She was safeguarding herself because she didn't trust him. Will deserved a woman who held a higher opinion of him.

Becca fiddled with the straw in her iced tea. "You have to understand where she's coming from."

The hell I do.

"Take it from another single mom, divorce leaves us fragile."

"You are about as fragile as steel rebar."

She beamed. "I'd like to think I handle my vulnerabilities better than some. But it makes sense that she's hesitant to put her and her children in the position to be hurt again. Would you say Tasha breaking up with you had any lasting effects?"

He recalled the unexpected swell of bitterness during his tuxedo fitting. "Yeah."

"So imagine the scars you would have if that breakup came after years of marriage. It's even worse if you feel betrayed because your husband was a dishonest son of a bitch." She said it matter-of-factly, but there was lingering pain in her eyes. When her husband skipped town with stolen money, no one had been more appalled or angry than Becca.

"Megan's husband did lie to her," he said slowly.

If there was one person in the world that you should be able to trust, shouldn't it be your spouse? Yet Spencer had deceived and manipulated her. Maybe the problem was not her distrusting Will but herself. After being wrong before, how was she supposed to gauge when a man would keep his vows? *Especially since you never got around to making any.* Megan hadn't given him the chance to tell her he loved her.

Because she was scared. She'd been afraid that Will wouldn't be there for her and her daughters, that he wouldn't stick around. So the best way to prove his feelings was to do exactly that—stay put and show her he wouldn't be run off at the first sign of trouble.

"Becca, I'm not a quitter."

"So you keep saying," she said with a twinkle in her eye. "Don't tell me. Go tell her."

TRYING TO LOSE herself in work, Megan was typing up an inventory supply order while Dagmar listed things they needed to restock. Megan almost never worked this late, but the triplets had been invited by a friend from preschool to a movie tonight. She'd much rather be here in the shop than home alone, torturing herself with peeks out her window to see if women were coming and going from Will's house.

She'd reacted like a complete lunatic when she saw him hugging that blonde earlier in the week. For starters, it had looked like a friendly embrace. Hardly evidence that they'd just finished having mad, passionate sex. Besides, even if they had, she'd forfeited the right to be upset about it. But what had truly gutted her in that moment was looking across the driveway and realizing how much *she* wanted to be in Will's arms. She was torn up over her decision to stop seeing him, and the triplets weren't helping—constantly asking when he was going to come over and have dinner with them again or wanting to make him new art projects. *That kind of attachment is exactly why you had to give him up, so the girls don't get overly invested.*

I did the right thing. Maybe.

Well, her mother certainly believed Megan was in the right. Of course, Beth Ann had also believed Megan should have stayed married to a serial cheater, so what did she know?

Megan suspected that Kate Sullivan Trent was not thrilled with her decision, but since her friend was gone on her honeymoon, Megan didn't have to face her yet. She heaved a sigh, wondering if she should get Dagmar's opinion.

"Can I ask you something?"

"Of course, mouse. You— Oh my." Dagmar glanced past the desk toward the front of the store, her eyes huge.

"What is it?" The bell hadn't rung, so nobody had entered the shop.

"I…just realized that I may have left my stove on at lunchtime. I'd better get straight home and check. Lock up when you leave," she called, already scurrying toward the exit, her coat hanging off one arm as she grabbed her purse.

She was in such a rush that Megan almost believed the stove excuse. Except that, if she wasn't mistaken, her aunt had been smiling. She rose from the desk and followed after Dagmar to investigate. Her aunt hurried out of the store, nearly bowling over Will Trent, who was on his way in. She'd obviously seen him through the floor-to-ceiling window looking out on Main Street.

Megan swallowed. Was he coming here specifically to see her? She didn't want to jump to conclusions. It was just as likely that he was running an errand for Gayle. Or, for all she knew, maybe Captain Hooper had decided the station house could use some floral touches.

He stepped inside, and their eyes locked. She gripped the counter, feeling faint. "Will." She'd meant to sound composed and cordial, but the word came out a breathy plea. For what, forgiveness? She didn't blame him for being angry with her. Was she making an unconscious appeal for a second chance? Because nothing had changed since Christmas Eve. *That's not entirely true. Now you have a more concrete idea of how miserable you are without him.*

Exactly. She was even more painfully aware of the risks.

"I'm here to order flowers," he told her from the other side of the counter.

So it was a professional reason, not a personal one. The disappointment was so staggering she nearly lost her balance. She swallowed hard. "Of course. What kind?"

"I don't know." He reached out and covered her hand with his. "What are your favorite flowers?"

"You want me to make a recommendation?" Her throat burned. She was surprised to realize she hadn't pulled her hand away yet, but his touch was almost like an anchor, keeping her paradoxically steady even as he was the reason she felt adrift.

"I want to order flowers *for* you." He gave her a lopsided smile. "It may be tacky to have you make your own bouquet, but there's no other florist in Cupid's Bow."

"I don't understand," she whispered.

He let go of her hand, and the loss was acute. But then he rounded the counter, coming toward her. Her heart thundered so loudly in her ears it was amazing she could still hear him.

"I don't know what your favorite flowers are, Megan, but I want to. There are so many things I want to discover about you, if you'll give us that chance."

She bit her lip, so tempted to say yes. Was succumbing to him smart, or merely self-indulgent?

"But there are some things I know for sure about you," he continued. "I know you're a fantastic mother who'd do just about anything for her kids. I know that you hate mushrooms, that you're a terrific cook despite a regrettable tendency to sneak broccoli into food, that you're strong and self-reliant, that you have a wicked sense of humor. I know your kisses make me crazy, I know how you taste when you're turned on. And I know that you deserve a strong man who will love you and only you. I'm that man, Megan."

She pressed a hand to her midsection, trying to catch her breath, reeling from his declaration. A tear slid over her cheek, and she realized it wasn't the first one.

"I do love you," he repeated softly. "I know those words aren't a magical guarantee. I'd give you one if I could, but that's not how life works. Still, I'm willing to earn your trust. If you really don't want me, say it and I'll go. But if there's a chance that—"

"Don't go." She clutched at his hand. What was an abstract, possible future pain compared to the absolute certainty of devastation if he walked out the door right now?

He was right, life didn't come with guarantees. But, judging by how his words had made her feel, it came with miraculous happiness. You just had to be brave enough to take the risk. Her mother had tried to convince her to stay in a bad marriage because she'd been afraid single life would be too hard. What did Megan want to cling to—fearful resignation, or courageous joy?

She took a deep breath. "I love you, too." Despite her past hurts, despite her fears, the words weren't hard to say at all. They tumbled out freely, and as soon as she'd said them she felt relieved, lighter. Ecstatic.

He crushed her against him for a hungry kiss, and her happy tears dampened both of their faces.

"I'm sorry," she murmured across his lips. "So sorry…"

Pressing his forehead to hers, he smiled down at her. "Quit apologizing, woman, and kiss me back."

She did, fervently. With a groan, he dropped his hands to her butt and pulled her closer. Need sizzled between them, but she couldn't act on it in front of the window for all of Cupid's Bow to see. A Mistletoe Moment was one thing; Florist In Flagrante was quite another.

"What if I lock up early?" she asked, nipping at his bottom lip. "And give you a tour of the back?"

He straightened. "You know, I have *always* wanted to see the back of a flower shop."

"Then it's about to be your lucky day."

"ARM'S LENGTH," WILL called across the dark yard. "Make sure you hold the sparkler at arm's length, Luke. And when it goes out—"

"We know," Jace interrupted with a groan. He set his beer on the deck railing and gave Megan a long-suffering look. "Can't you make out with him and distract him from boring us with the same safety lectures he gives every year? We get it—wear the gloves, put the extinguished sparklers in the bucket of water, only let children over the age of five hold one."

Megan's triplets didn't seem upset over not handling sparklers. Lily and Iris were happily coloring with Alyssa at the picnic table, beneath the glow of tiki lanterns and twinkle lights. Daisy was down in the yard with Luke and Mandy, but the attention from the older kids seemed to be more of a draw than the sparklers. They'd all gathered in the backyard of Kate and Cole's new house to celebrate New Year's Eve. The newlyweds were barely moved in, all of their belongings still in boxes, but Cole said they'd have a decent view of the town fireworks display.

Will put his arm around her and tugged her against his side. "You heard the man. Care to make out with me and prevent me from being tedious?"

"You are never tedious. But I'm happy to make out with you anyway." She reached up to press her mouth to his, a soul-deep sense of belonging filling her. Behind her, Alyssa and Iris giggled, reminding her that they had an audience. "Maybe we should find a darker corner."

"Maybe we should leave immediately after the fireworks," Will whispered against her ear, "and make sure the girls are asleep well before midnight. I have very specific ideas on how I want to ring in the New Year."

She blushed, hoping it was too dark for Will's family to notice. "You're good with holidays. You made the girls' Christmas season magical, and this is the best New Year's Eve ever."

"Just wait until you see what I have in store for you on Valentine's Day." He winked at her. "And on Saint Patrick's Day. And the Cupid's Bow Centennial. And International Talk Like a Pirate Day. And Arbor Day!"

She laughed but knew that beneath the silliness of his words was a promise. They had a future together, countless holidays to share and memories to build. He stood by his word, and he would stand by her, loving her faithfully—even at her most prickly.

Kate glanced across the deck and raised her glass of wine in an unspoken toast to their happiness. "Remind me, who caught my bridal bouquet, again?"

As recently as last week, Megan would have blustered that she didn't know if she'd ever remarry, that she was certainly in no hurry to jeopardize her heart again. Now she merely smiled, snuggling against the man she loved, basking in hope and possibilities.

* * * * *

Be sure to look for more CUPID'S BOW, TEXAS, *stories by Tanya Michaels in 2017!*

MILLS & BOON®

Cherish™

EXPERIENCE THE ULTIMATE RUSH OF FALLING IN LOVE

Just can't wait?
Buy our books online a month before they hit the shops!
www.millsandboon.co.uk

Also available as eBooks.

MILLS & BOON®

EXCLUSIVE EXTRACT

Crown Prince Armando enlists Rosa Lamberti to find
him a suitable wife—but could a stolen kiss under the
mistletoe lead to an unexpected Christmas wedding?

Read on for a sneak preview of
WINTER WEDDING FOR THE PRINCE
by Barbara Wallace

"Have you ever looked at an unfocused telescope only
to turn the knob and make everything sharp and clear?"
Armando asked.

Rosa nodded.

"That is what it was like for me, a few minutes ago.
One moment I had all these sensations I couldn't
explain swirling inside me, then the next everything
made sense. They were my soul coming back to life."

"I don't know what to think," she said.

"Then don't think," he replied. "Just go with your
heart."

He made it sound easy. Just go with your heart. But
what if your heart was frightened and confused? For
all his talk of coming to life, he was essentially in the
same place as before, unable or unwilling to give her
a true emotional commitment.

On the other hand, her feelings wanted to override
her common sense, so maybe they were even. As she
watched him close the gap between them, she felt her
heartbeat quicken to match her breath.

"You do know that we're under the mistletoe yet again, don't you?"

The sprig of berries had quite a knack for timing, didn't it? Anticipation ran down her spine ceasing what little hold common sense still had. Armando was going kiss her and she was going to let him. She wanted to lose herself in his arms. Believe for a moment that his heart felt more than simple desire.

This time, when he wrapped his arm around her waist, she slid against him willingly, aligning her hips against his with a smile.

"Appears to be our fate," she whispered. "Mistletoe, that is."

"You'll get no complaints from me." She could hear her heart beating in her ears as his head dipped toward hers. "Merry Christmas, Rosa."

"Mer..." His kiss swallowed the rest of her wish. Rosa didn't care if she spoke another word again. She'd waited her whole life to be kissed like this. Fully and deeply, with a need she felt all the way down to her toes.

They were both breathless when the moment ended. With their foreheads resting against each other, she felt Armando smile against her lips. "Merry Christmas," he whispered again.

Don't miss
WINTER WEDDING FOR THE PRINCE
by Barbara Wallace

Available December 2016

www.millsandboon.co.uk

MILLS & BOON®

Why shop at millsandboon.co.uk?

Each year, thousands of romance readers find their perfect read at millsandboon.co.uk. That's because we're passionate about bringing you the very best romantic fiction. Here are some of the advantages of shopping at www.millsandboon.co.uk:

* **Get new books first**—you'll be able to buy your favourite books one month before they hit the shops

* **Get exclusive discounts**—you'll also be able to buy our specially created monthly collections, with up to 50% off the RRP

* **Find your favourite authors**—latest news, interviews and new releases for all your favourite authors and series on our website, plus ideas for what to try next

* **Join in**—once you've bought your favourite books, don't forget to register with us to rate, review and join in the discussions

Visit **www.millsandboon.co.uk**
for all this and more today!